Flying Lessons

Flying Lessons

Karen Hood-Caddy

RENDEZVOUS
PRESS

Cover photography by
Jim Flynn, Photography as Art Wild Life Photos

Published by RendezVous Press
Napoleon Publishing/RendezVous Press
Toronto, Ontario, Canada
www.rendezvouspress.com

Printed in Canada

05 04 03 02 01   5 4 3 2 1

Canadian Cataloguing in Publication Data

Hood-Caddy, Karen, date
Flying lessons

ISBN 0-929141-80-6

I. Title.

PS8565.06514F59 2001   C813'.54   C2001-930218-5
PR9199.3.H66F59 2001

To Stanley
And to my son, Jason
And all lovers of wild things

For inspiration, thanks to my unmet heroes: Julia Cameron, Dian Fossey*, John Irving, Annie LaMott, Margaret Laurence, Hilda Murrell*, Laurens Van der Post, Karen Silkwood* and David Suzuki.

For help in the various aspects of birthing a novel, my heartfelt appreciations to: Martin Avery, Cheryl Cooper, Sue Dean, Cindy Frewer, Kathyann Johnston, Kathy Cahill-Kuntz, Mel Malton, Jack Martin, Sylvia McConnell, Sallie Onley, Robert Rea, Craig Rintoul, Theresa Sansome, Richard Scrimger, Stanley Sharman, Antanas Sileika and Allister Thompson and Gary Wood.

And much gratitude for the support of: Jason Caddy, Ron and Mary Doty, Marlena Field, Lizzy Gilbert, Karen Graham, Elaine Hassard, Jim Hood, Gaile Hood, Kevin Kelly, Richard Onley, Caroline Robertson, Stan Tait, Linda Wright and all the people who have been in my courses or hired me as a coach.

I also wish to acknowledge Michael and Janice Enright who run A Wing and A Prayer, the Muskoka Centre for Wild Birds. The essentials of the loon stories portrayed in this book are based on birds they helped return to the wild. They can be contacted at: jenright@primus.ca Thanks too to Dr. George Collard, veterinarian, who has helped them and me.

Lastly, special appreciation to The Holiday Inn (Aston Villa) resort. I have spent many wonderful hours writing there and consider their decks to be some of the finest in Muskoka.

* These women all had their lives taken in ecological battles

There are two lasting bequests
we can give our children.
One is roots, the other is wings.

-Hodding Carter Jr.

All the darkness in the world
can't extinguish the light
of one candle.

-Anonymous

Chapter 1

Muskoka. The word skimmed the surface of Jessie's sleep like a broad-winged gull. She opened her eyes with a start. Through the window, she could see a God-sized handful of elephant grey rock and a green tufted jack pine, wind-blown and wild.

Relieved, she shifted her gaze to the honey-coloured walls of her bedroom, saw the poetry book on her night table, the notes for her thesis scattered on the floor. Yes, she was still here, in Muskoka, not in the hospital. Not yet. Drowsiness tugged at her eyes, and she felt herself drifting down. Then a dream capsized her, and she was floating in the silent belly of the lake. Around her, the water was green and golden, and she felt safe and succoured by it, like a child in the arms of a grandparent.

Beside her, Harley moved and she awoke again. Apprehension clutched at her stomach. Turning, she curled her back into the comforting swell of Harley's plentiful body. How could anyone have a belly so warm? In the distance, she could hear the long hoot of the train over by Mactier. Usually she couldn't hear the early morning train, but it had rained in the night and the moisture in the air was billowing the sound out, making it huge with reverberation. Love did this too, she thought. Expanded you, made you big. When she'd first fallen in love with Harley, her heart had felt as big as an air balloon.

And her whole body had felt swollen, probably was swollen, she thought, her attraction to him had been so intense.

As much as she liked the sound of the train, she didn't like its message. It was seven-fifteen. That meant she only had three hours left. Three hours until her date with a scalpel in Toronto.

Harley put his full mouth on the bare skin of her shoulder and pulled her close. "I could still come with you and do ceremony."

She smiled, imagining him bringing sweet grass and smudging her hospital room. As much as she'd like that, Harley and his native traditions belonged in the city like elk in the subway.

"I'd rather think of you here." It would be fortifying to think of him near the lake and trees.

Harley brought his face close. "Scared?"

Emotions thickened her throat, squeezing out the possibility of words. Harley's huge hands stroked her forehead. His hands gave care.

Refuge. When her breath eased, he planted large-mouthed kisses over her chest, then brought his face close. She looked into his eyes. They were as dark and peaceful as the woods. There for her to walk into.

She pulled him on top of her and she could feel his hesitation. He looked at her questioningly, but she spread herself open. She wanted every part of him in contact with every part of her. He closed his eyes, and she watched him. There was something so innocent and pure about pleasure. She loved the way it made his face flush. When he opened his eyes, her own fell into his as if through doors suddenly opened. She loved this, the way he let her penetrate him here, while he penetrated her below. It made a circle. A circle that began to spin and whirl. She concentrated on the sensations, pressing them into her memory like photographs into an album she might take with her.

A low growl came from Harley's throat. She felt him pause, hold back. Thinking she was too tense for this release herself, she urged him on. But Harley moved until she felt a sweet heat erupt through her pelvis. She cried out. As she did, Harley arched his head up as if he was about to receive some sort of celestial benediction and gripped her shoulder, holding his body taut, clenching the sensations as they moved through him, quenching his body in the fullness of them. His face was bright with awe. Then, the brightness faded and he eased himself down over top of her, puppy slack and happy.

"Sometimes you know me better than I know myself," she said after a while.

Harley kissed her and got up.

Jessie rubbed her foot. It took so much energy to deal with pain. And she didn't have much energy. Not after another poor night's sleep.

"You had that dream again," Harley said, pulling on a pair of faded jeans.

"Did I shout?"

Harley put a finger in his ear and wiggled it.

"Sorry…"

He silenced her with another kiss.

The dream was always the same. She and a group of people were sleeping in a house while some sort of catastrophe happened outside. She'd awaken and begin to shout at everyone to wake up, wake up. But as loud and as hard as she shouted, she wasn't able to wake them.

As if she might leave the dream in the bed, Jessie pulled back the covers and stood. Harley took her arms and wrapped them around his neck and picked her up, piggy-backing her past the small cabin where he did his leatherwork, down the earth pathway to the lake. Almost at the grey dock, beside where they kept the little tin boat, he stopped walking and nodded towards a turtle sunning itself on a rock near the water.

She smiled. She loved turtles. Harley believed the turtle was his totem.

"Eagle Eyes!" she whispered. When Harley was around, wild things were never far away. "How come you always see things first?"

His mouth curved with amusement.

"Remind me to put that in the book," she said as he set her down.

A year ago, she'd started recording what she saw in nature: the first ruby-throated humming bird, where the wild garlic was, when the trilliums cartwheeled down the hill by the river. It made her feel good every time she wrote an entry. It was as if by recording what she saw, she could reassure herself that the trout lilies, the song sparrows, the otters, were all still alive and well.

She eased herself down into the forest green Muskoka chair and looked out over the lake. The sun had turned the surface into a pool of molten silver. The flash of it was so bright, so beautiful, it made her eyes sting. She looked up into the open-armed sky.

"I thank you God for most this amazing day: for the leaping greenly spirits of trees and a blue true dream of sky..."

As she recited the poem, she looked over at Harley, but he was striding over to pick up something that was bobbing in the water by the side of the dock. He held up the Coke can for her to see.

Jessie frowned. "I can't stand it."

They often found things like this floating in the lake. It was ridiculous. Harley threw the can in a box he kept for such things, then sat beside her.

He scanned the lake. "It's peaceful."

From the serenity on Harley's face, she knew he had moved past the Coke can, but she hadn't. She still felt annoyed.

"No jet-ski," he added.

For the past few days, some kid had been out on one for hours. Jessie hated it when anyone monopolized the lake like that. The lake was for everybody: fish, ducks, turtles, birds, not just boats. And especially not jet-skis. Her friend Elfy said they sounded like souped-up chain saws. Jessie thought Elfy was being complimentary.

Above them, an attenuated V of Canada geese was flying, their long necks straight as arrows, their huge six-foot wings whooshing as they pumped the air. Her hand leapt to her chest. She loved birds, all birds, but to her, geese were miraculous. As she stood admiring them, the geese began to honk, and she waved up at them.

Beside her, Harley was still.

"What?" She nudged him with her arm. When Harley was this still, she knew something was wrong.

He stared up into the sky. "Something's not right."

"What?" There was irritation in her voice. She didn't want there to be "something not right". Not this morning. Why did he have to say these things? "How do you know?"

Harley kneeled. Dipping his fingers in the water, he

drew a series of concentric circles on the dry dock. "We're here," he said, pointing to the innermost circle. "When something happens here," he moved his finger to the outside ring, "the birds and animals talk. The ones in the next ring hear, then they talk and the ones in the next ring hear. The news gets passed on…" He moved his finger ring by ring to the centre.

"So, that's how the Indians used to know when white men were coming."

Harley nodded.

Jessie scrutinized the way the geese were flying as they made their way across the sky. She didn't see anything unusual. But then her clients often didn't know how she was able to figure out so much about them just from the way they walked into the room.

She sighed. "As long as whatever's 'not right' doesn't have anything to do with me."

Harley viewed her pitifully, then bumped her with his hip. She teetered, grabbed at his arm, but he slipped it out of her grasp, and she fell into the water.

"Harley!"

She didn't mind, but she wasn't going to let Harley think she didn't.

Pleased with himself, Harley ignored the water she splashed at him and dove in. Charlie, their golden lab, jumped in after and a crown of water erupted out of the surface of the lake.

Jessie swam up the shore. The water felt cool and clean against her body, almost silky. When she'd swum far enough, she turned over and pulled her arms through the water, sweeping them from over her head to her waist. It was like making angel wings. The sun warmed her face and caught the water droplets in her eyelashes, making everything sparkle. She stopped swimming and let the water hold her up. As she floated, it lapped over her skin. An acute feeling of contentment moved through her chest. There was something so magical about water. It soothed and healed and brought her home to herself.

What was Canada doing, selling it to the highest bidder? It was ridiculous. Just because Canada had so much water didn't justify shipping trillions of gallons all over the world. She made a mental note to write a letter to the Minister of Natural Resources. Then she remembered that she still had that letter to write about the Endangered Species legislation. And that petition about the CBC to sign.

She grimaced. Couldn't she have a day off? A day when she didn't have to monitor the well-being of the world? What did she think? That without her vigilant eye, the world would spin out of orbit? Just how self-important could a person get?

The problem was, every time she listened to the news, there was another ecological calamity. If she heard of one more species becoming extinct, being exterminated was more like it, she was going to, she was going to—what? Throw up? Throw a fit? Throw a grenade?

Normally, she thought of herself as a reasonable person. But even a reasonable person could be pushed too far. Although, sometimes, being pushed too far was what created change. She thought of one of her clients who had smoked two hundred cigarettes one weekend, making herself so sick of nicotine that she was able to amp up her resolve and actually quit. Taking things to the limit like this worked, but as a tool for change, it wasn't very elegant.

Self-induced shock therapy is what it was.

As she floated on her back, she felt tired. She wondered what it would be like to not move, just to let the lake take her into itself. Virginia Woolf had died by putting stones in her pockets and submerging herself. That beat dying in a hospital. Or getting slowly poisoned to death with chemotherapy. That's what was happening to one of her cousins. Goodness, if she had to go through that, she'd drown herself for sure. No, if she were going to die, she wanted to face death valiantly, not run from it like a frightened rodent.

She paddled her hands so she was floating again. Was she going to die today? She didn't think so. Her surgery wasn't life threatening, but, still, the unexpected could happen. Not everyone died peacefully in their beds at the age of ninety-two. In fact, hardly anyone did. It was just another of the illusions people fabricated to shield themselves from fear. Fear. Of all the emotions, it was the most taboo.

Last night when she'd told Aggie she was scared of going into the hospital, Aggie had said, "Don't be silly!"

Of all the emotions, it was probably the most powerful, Jessie thought. In a way, it ran the world. It certainly fuelled the economy. If people weren't frightened about being good enough, for example, they wouldn't care about what they wore or what kind of car they drove. If people weren't afraid, they wouldn't care how much money they made either.

Yet, in a strange way, most people liked fear. Not a lot of fear, but just enough to get their insides tingling. People liked to make others feel afraid too. Never had she heard as many horror stories about medical mishaps as she had in the last few weeks. Just last night Aggie had related in detail the mistake her doctor had made with her medication. Thank you, Aggie. Just what I needed to hear. But, just because bad things *could* happen didn't mean they *would* happen, and if she was going to continue hiking in the woods, her foot surgery was necessary.

Gathering her resolve for all she had ahead of her, Jessie swam back. At the dock, Harley gave her his hand and pulled her dripping body up and into his arms. She kissed his mouth in thanks. His lips tasted of the lake. She pressed herself against him as if the very warmth of him could protect her from anything bad ever happening.

•   •   •

In Toronto, an alarm clock fired off its sound like a gun at the starting gate. Alex pushed herself up. Don't think. Don't feel. Just get your ass in gear. *Damn*, her throat hurt. Ignore it, she told herself and reached for some pills. KILLS PAIN FAST, the bottle said. Do it, pills: kill.

Alex slashed the shower curtain aside and saw the grey ring around the bathtub. Shit. She *hated* this. Why was it so difficult to get a cleaning lady who actually cleaned? Double shit. No cleanser. Pushing herself on, she hefted a load of laundry down to the kitchen. The machine was already half full of clothes. Sometimes she was sure her kids tossed things in the washing machine just to avoid putting them away. She stuffed more in anyway and punched the start button. There was an odd, grinding sound. She ignored it and forged on.

Switching on the coffee maker, she looked for waffles. She had to do something to make it up to Christina.

Although Tom *had* filmed Christina's play with the camcorder, and Alex had every intention of watching it tonight when she got home, Christina was in a snit about her missing it. Her own parents had seldom shown up at her school events. And if Christina was going to keep her whopping clothing allowance and membership in the tennis club, *someone* had to pay for it all.

Damn. No waffles. English muffins would have to do. She shoved two into the toaster oven and strode outside for the paper. Why couldn't the paperboy throw the damn thing on the porch? It only took a minute to get it, but a minute every day added up to three hundred and sixty-five minutes a year. That was six whole hours. She could set up two, maybe three, million-dollar portfolios in six hours.

Evan's five-hundred-dollar mountain bike lay on the lawn in the rain. She gathered her breath for a full-fledged shout.

"Ev—"

Pain sliced off the sound like a meat cleaver.

Fuming, she tramped across the manicured lawn and escorted the bike to the garage. Across the street, Mr. Rutledge stepped into his chauffeur-driven limousine. She ducked behind a tree. Why couldn't Tom make that kind of money?

Inside the house, she bounded up the stairs two at a time to get some aerobics in and collided with her daughter. Christina was wearing a long white T-shirt with a screaming face on it. Her daughter had drawn the face herself.

"Can I?" Christina regarded her with rumpled, fourteen-year-old disdain.

Kids! They were always at you. Wanting this,

demanding that. Once upon a time, Christina had silky hair the colour of dark honey, exactly like Alex's. Then she'd stuck her head in a peroxide bottle. Her hair was now chalk white and wound into dreadlocks as thick as rope. Yesterday, she'd started lobbying for some red streaks.

"We'll talk about it later," Alex said.

"It's *my* hair," Christina shouted.

But it came from me, Alex wanted to scream. Didn't that count for anything? Why was every interaction with her daughter a wrestling match? Last week they'd fought over whether Christina could have a tattoo. A tattoo!

Alex pushed past her daughter and went into the bathroom. Why had she ever agreed to allow Christina to stay home the extra night? Both her children went to boarding schools and normally went back on Sunday evenings, but Christina had a birthday party to go to and Alex had given in. Then, of course, Evan had wanted to stay too. When she'd said no, his damned wheezing had started, and she'd had to find his inhaler. God, she hated that thing. It made her feel flawed. Should she take Evan to another specialist? Tom said Evan had wheezed all the way back to school last night. What was the matter with him? Other kids would kill to go to St. Andrew's.

7.19! Alex took a quick shower and brushed on a coat of Hard as Nails. The smell of it pinched her nostrils. Where were her tweezers? Christina had been into her cosmetics again. This time, Alex was going to fine her. Not that Christina cared. "Whatever," she'd said the last time and tossed some coins on the table. *Whatever.* Alex couldn't *stand* that word, and Christina knew it.

On her dressing table was a photo of Christina, at age ten, holding Alex's briefcase in one hand and a cell phone in the other. Pretending to be "Mommy" had been one of Christina's favourite games. When had it all changed? How had Alex become the enemy? Alex's friends told her this was normal, part of Christina becoming her own person, but she couldn't stand it. Would it have been different if she had stayed home with the kids? Maybe if she'd given in to motherhood more, not had all those nannies. Maybe if she'd gone to that stupid play last night...

Hands found her breasts. She gave Tom a quick peck on the cheek and stood up, pulling away.

Tom held on. "Your breasts are pleading with me to take them to the bedroom."

"You wish."

Tom's eyebrow arched at the croak of her voice, and he raised his hand to her forehead. She slipped away. In a few minutes she was dressed and in the kitchen, heating up the muffins, putting bacon on the grill, getting the coffee percolating, the juicer juicing, the kettle boiling and the blender blending. She had more than twenty appliances, all the colour of champagne. As she moved from one to the other, the washing machine made a diabolical sound. She turned to see a swollen lip of suds rise up under the lid of the machine and disgorge all over the kitchen floor.

In the doorway, Christina stood, her arms folded across her chest.

"Way to go, Mom."

Chapter 2

Wrapped in a towel, Jessie sat between Harley's legs in the big green Muskoka chair and leaned against his chest. In the distance, they could see a small figure paddling a pale yellow canoe towards them.

"That paddling arm of hers is getting weaker and weaker," Harley said as they watched Elfy approach.

Jessie grimaced. She didn't want to hear this. Elfy was well into her seventies and, until this year, had the energy of a wind-up toy. Lately, however, she'd been moving slower and slower.

"All right, you two, break it up," Elfy called when the canoe was closer.

Jessie smiled. "Goodness, Elfy, if we had half the sex life you imagine—"

"Imagining's all a person's got at my age." She pushed her Toronto Blue Jays cap back on her ginger-coloured hair and looked at Jessie. "Feel ready?"

"Ready as I'll ever be."

"Sure you don't want me to drive you down?"

Jessie shook her head. Was Elfy forgetting?

"Oh, yeah," Elfy said. "I don't *have* a car anymore." She laughed. "That's the crazy thing about getting old. You forget that you forget." She pushed up the sleeves of her hornet yellow sweatshirt and waved grandly to the other seat in the canoe. "Let me drive you around the bay then."

Thinking it would be a good distraction, Jessie stood up and pulled on a bathing suit under her towel. "Only if that jet-ski stays off the lake. It just about drove me nuts yesterday."

"Made me grateful for this, for once." Elfy pointed to her hearing aid. She watched Jessie hobble towards the boat. "Foot sore, eh?"

"Yup."

A puckish smile pulled at Elfy's mouth. "If you'd only stop kicking people…"

"I've tried stopping, but the people in my Kickers Anonymous group say it's going to take time." Jessie's foot kicked out as if she couldn't control it.

"Maybe you should see a therapist."

Jessie hooted with laughter. The old woman knew how to hit the bull's eye.

"Not that there're any good ones around here."

"Look at all the therapy you've had, and it hasn't helped you," Jessie said.

Elfy grinned and shrugged. "Tried sanity once. Bor-ring!"

"Five minutes isn't long enough, Elf." Harley said.

"Hey, what happened to Charlie?" She pointed to the scratch beneath the dog's eye. "Cat?"

Jessie looked at the old woman. Her face was as brown and crinkled as an old paper bag. "Don't know."

"Damn cats!"

"Crank it up, Elf, crank it up." Harley smiled and rolled his eyes. He could tell she was gearing up for one of her famous harangues about cats.

"Can't help it. Seen more mangled birds at the refuge…"

For over a year now, Elfy had been volunteering at the

bird refuge which was on the property next to Jessie's. As a result of seeing all the damage cats did to birds, she and Maggie, the woman who ran the refuge, had been lobbying the local councillors to pass a cat leashing law. Jessie had no doubt they would make it happen. When Elfy set her mind to something, there was usually no stopping her.

"What do you call a bunch of cats chained to the bottom of the lake?" Elfy smirked as she pushed the canoe away from the dock. "A good start!"

"Oh, Elfy!" Jessie positioned an orange life jacket on the floor of the canoe for her knees and began paddling. They made their way past the buoy that marked some rocks a few hundred feet off shore and headed towards Bird Island. She lifted her binoculars and viewed the hundreds of seagulls and herons that were nesting there. The sight of them filled her with satisfaction. Although it had taken years, she and Maggie and some other bird lovers had succeeded in having the island designated as a bird sanctuary. That meant the birds now had a place of their own, free from human activity, to nest and procreate.

As they paddled out of the bay, Wildwood came into view. Of all the lodges in Muskoka, this was the one she loved best. Nestled in a forest black-green with magnificent pines, the rustic old lodge was made of foot-square logs and field stones. Built over a hundred years ago, it was renowned for a tall totem pole that stood at its front entrance. Rumour had it that an Ojibway medicine man had put the totem pole there to mark it as a sacred place. As a child Jessie had been fascinated by the totem pole, imagining that the various faces were telling her things.

"Take your pictures now," Elfy said. "Before the new

owner gets at it with some fancy-pants designer from the city. Old Archie better be buried deep."

Archie Anderson, bless him, had been careful to keep Wildwood's old-world charm, despite the fact that palatial condominiums with glitzy dining rooms, hot tubs and tennis courts were going up throughout the area. But Archie had died over a year ago and left the five hundred acre property to a cousin. Rumours were rife about what the new owner, Dick Price, was going to do. Already he'd applied to the town to build several new docks.

"Maybe the guy's going to start a jet-ski school." Elfy smirked.

Jessie groaned. "You'd have to lock me up."

"Prison or insane asylum?"

"Depends on whether the cops got me before or after I'd shot him."

"Right," Elfy said. "But I tell you, Maggie's knickers are sure in a knot. She says it's only a matter of time till we all get the boot. Says she can hear it in the bird calls."

Jessie's stomach tightened. Like herself and Harley, Maggie rented from the Wildwood estate. When Archie was alive, the security of their tenancy had never been an issue. As often as not, Jessie had to take her rent over to him, or he would have forgotten about it entirely. He often refused outright to take Maggie's money. He loved birds and knew Maggie was running the refuge on a shoestring.

"The last time I talked to Archie," Jessie said, "he promised the rental agreements would be honoured."

Elfy grimaced. "Can't do much from six feet under."

Jessie sighed. Archie had the head of a watermelon when it came to business. "Oh, Elfy…" She didn't want to think about this. Not now.

"It's Price's son who's been out there on the jet-ski, you know."

"DJ?" Jessie frowned.

"You know him?"

"Let's just say I've heard of him."

A few months before, one of the local guidance councillors had asked if she had any time to assess a kid, a service she sometimes did for the school. "This one could be trouble," Jack Dempsey had warned. "You know the story. Big-wig dad who's got no time for his son. So he buys the kid toys. Cars. Computers. Gives the kid everything but what he really needs—a bit of discipline and love. The kid's smart, but he's also a smartass, mouths off at everyone. Frankly, I think he's just royally pissed off at his family and is taking it out on everyone. Last week he showed up drunk. Or stoned. Never did figure out which."

"You can't always sometimes tell," Jessie quipped, then told Jack she'd see him. "Set it up and let me know."

But when Jessie had arrived at the school for her first appointment with him, DJ hadn't shown up. After he stood her up a second time, she'd bowed out. She had too many clients who wanted to see her to justify waiting around for a recalcitrant kid.

Jessie watched her paddle move through the water, making it dimple and swirl.

"By the way, has anyone heard anything about Price's dock application?" She, Elfy and some others who were opposed to it had sent in a letter of protest to the Town, arguing that the construction of the docks would destroy valuable shoreline. As any long-term resident of Muskoka knew, shoreline was vitally important for the survival of nearly all wildlife and the area had already suffered significant losses.

"Nope. Can't for the life of me see why he wants so many boat slips."

"Neither can I," Jessie said.

"Maybe it's time for the Grannies," Elfy said. "It's been a while since they've had something to sink their teeth into."

The Grannies were a group of seniors Elfy had organized a few years before to help Jessie in a campaign to save a stand of hundred-year-old trees. The incident had received a lot of press, and ever since, Jessie hadn't been able to walk down the street without someone accosting her. Some people patted her on the back, others told her off. It didn't really matter which—both actions made her feel as if she were in a state of siege. "My life's just getting back to normal!"

"Normal! You want normal? Normal is shopping malls and Pop Tarts!"

"I've never eaten a Pop Tart in my life!"

Elfy pressed her thin lips together and paddled on. "See that thing on TV about the floods down south?"

Jessie shook her head. She was aware that there had been severe flooding in the Carolinas, but that was all.

"The houses had water up to the windows," Elfy said. "'Course, they evacuated the people, put them in shelters, but they left all the pets. The cats I didn't mind, but the dogs! Pretty near broke my heart to see those dogs left like that. Anyways, this woman didn't want to see them die either, so she went around in a little motor boat and rescued them. Took them home to her place and cared for them until their owners were able to get them."

"Why am I imagining this is going to have an unhappy ending?"

Elf flicked the water from her paddle at Jessie. "'Cause it does. One of the woman's neighbours blabbed to the town, and she got slapped with a thousand dollar fine for breaking some stupid bylaw." She stopped paddling. "Maybe I'm too old."

"What's age got to do with it?"

"You get impatient."

"I feel impatient sometimes."

Elfy pointed at some rocks tinged with green. "For crying out loud, look at that slime!"

Jessie didn't want to look. It filled her with anguish to see nature being violated, but by not looking, she would be perpetuating her own denial, and that was far more dangerous. She looked at the rock Elfy was pointing at. A sick feeling moved up her throat.

"Makes me want to park myself at Earth First's door. Tell them to use me like a spray can," Jessie said.

"They're the people who do all that radical stuff—"

"Radical by whose definition? If someone was forcing poison down your throat or trying to suffocate you, you wouldn't call it 'radical' if I tried to stop them? But if that life is a tree's or a river's, then it's somehow different. Then it becomes 'radical'."

"HA!" Elfy said. "We were called that and more during the tree campaign, weren't we? But anyone who's ever done anything gets names thrown at them. It's part of it. Toughens your skin."

"Then I should be an armadillo," Jessie said.

They steered the boat closer to shore, where the surface of the water was black and shiny. When they were deep in the bay, Jessie set her paddle across the gunnels and closed her eyes. Glad for a few moments of silence, she listened to the delicate sound of the water dripping from the paddle into the lake. The canoe rocked ever so gently beneath her and she felt the lazy stillness of the morning sun warm her skin. This was what she needed: some of nature's peace.

Then she heard a rustling.

Turning to where the sound was coming from, her breath caught in her throat.

"God have mercy!" Elfy said.

There, standing twenty feet away, was a goose, an arrow through its neck.

•　•　•

After Tom left to drive Christina to school, Alex forced more pills down her dry throat and slipped into her sleek black Jaguar. She ran her red-nailed fingers over the smooth, white leather seats. The car had been a present from her father for snagging the Royce account, and she always felt a surge of power driving it.

Leaving the tinted windows up and the air conditioner on high to cool her fever, she cruised along the shady residential streets, then turned on to the main road leading downtown. She pressed her two-hundred-dollar shoe more firmly onto the accelerator to increase her speed, but there was no response. Shit! She guided the stalled car over to the shoulder and turned the key. Click. Turned the key again. Click. Shit! Shit! SHIT!

Yanking her cell phone from her briefcase, she dialled her mechanic. After twenty-two rings, she hung up, pushed open the car door and tried to hail a cab. There wasn't one to be had. Grasping her briefcase securely under her arm, she strode towards the subway. She had a meeting with Oliver Silverman at nine sharp, and one did not keep a man of that stature waiting.

As she stepped onto the platform, a subway car arrived, and she pushed her way through the crowd. A person didn't get named "Business Woman of the Year" by being late. Or by staying home and coddling every sore throat that came along. She had to set an example. Show that women could cut it just as well as men. As her father said.

As the subway car began to move, the big-bodied woman in front of her gripped the overhead arm hold and swayed close. The woman was wearing a black leather miniskirt and the tabs from her garter belt came down beneath the skirt before hooking onto fish net stockings.

Ridiculous, Alex thought. Why couldn't the woman dress properly? If there was anything she couldn't stand, it was someone who didn't care what people thought. As if feeling her glare, the woman grinned down at her. That's when Alex noticed the "woman" had a beard. As if she'd been slapped, Alex's face spun away. The next time she looked, the man was scratching his balls. He had his hand under his skirt and was taking his time, like he was alone in his bathroom. Her palms started to sweat and little twitches jerked through her body. No, she couldn't have an anxiety attack. Not here. Not now! Opening her briefcase, she found her bottle of pain killers. Not having any water, she put a tablet in her mouth and chewed it. Aghh. That was bitter. She forced herself to swallow and picked up her daily planner.

There was a glut of meetings already penned in.

Usually this made her feel good, but at the moment, the entries looked like a bunch of squiggly hieroglyphics. A feeling of panic rose in her. Just at that moment, the train lurched forward and sped towards the next station. Alex clicked her briefcase shut and joined them.

• • •

The goose ruffled its wings and made agitated honking sounds.

"It's okay," Jessie said to it softly. "We won't hurt you."

The bird eyed them warily. Jessie frowned. No wonder it was frightened of them. One of her kind had just tried to kill it.

"Let's get it in the boat," Elfy whispered. "Take it to the refuge. That arrow has to come out."

Jessie nodded and they made their way in slowly. Closer now, she could see the arrow and the long, stainless-steel arrowhead that had pierced the middle of the bird's narrow black neck more clearly. Miraculously, the arrow must have missed both the wind pipe and the esophagus, or the bird wouldn't still be alive.

"Double trouble," Elfy said in a low voice.

Jessie turned sharply. A few hundred yards away, a second goose shifted its weight from one foot to the other.

"When one goose lands," Elfy said, "another always goes with it. They buddy each other up."

Jessie looked at the sharp, powerful beaks of the birds. Just last week she'd heard about a heron pecking a man in the eye. The bird's bill had penetrated the man's brain and killed him. "I don't want a beak in my face," she whispered.

"Me neither. But it's the wings you gotta watch. They're the bone busters."

"Maybe we should just—" What, leave it? As long as that arrow was in its neck, the goose wouldn't be able to feed itself, and if it couldn't eat, it would die. As scared as she was of what the goose might do, she couldn't stand the thought of leaving it.

Elfy took off her yellow sweatshirt. "I'll throw this over its head so it can't see. That will settle it down. Then we can lift it into the boat."

They beached the canoe further up the shore, then split up and circled behind the birds. As they closed in on the hurt one, the other one flapped its wings and squawked.

Jessie's heart jack-hammered against the front of her chest. "It's all right," she said, not sure if she was reassuring the goose or herself. As she neared the bird with the arrow, she could see the robust curve of its chest and the bright-white marking on the cheek of its ink-black head. Its breast and back were scalloped with layers of lustrous, brownish-grey feathers. Up close like this, the bird was truly magnificent. Why would anyone want to kill such beauty? Indignation swelled inside her.

They crept slowly forward, then Elfy lunged and threw her sweatshirt over the goose's head. The other bird made noises, but did not move.

"Keep those wings in!" Elfy warned as they lifted the goose into the boat.

"Easier said than—" This was one powerful bird, Jessie thought as she struggled to keep it on her lap. Behind them, she could hear the other goose honking its distress.

"Sorry, pal," Elfy called, digging her paddle into the

water. "We'll get her back as soon as we can."

Jessie hugged the bird firmly, and it settled down. She liked the feeling of it against her chest. She'd never been so close to a wild bird before and felt an awesome sense of privilege. Who had tried to kill it? The very thought made her stomach churn. In all her fifty-three years, she'd never done a violent act, but she knew she was capable. There were two things that pushed her to the edge of self-restraint: cruelty to children and cruelty to animals. Luckily, she'd never actually seen someone hurt a child or a wild thing, because she knew one thing for sure—she wouldn't stand by and let it happen.

As they paddled past Wildwood, the lines on Elfy's face deepened. "Bet that bonehead kid did this!"

Jessie didn't want to think about this. Not now. She closed her eyes and imagined the goose spreading its wings and flying away, far away. And in her fantasy, she flew away with it. She didn't want to be a part of a world where things like this happened.

When she looked up a few minutes later, she saw Harley standing on the dock. Without speaking a word, the three of them moved in unison, lifting the goose out of the boat and into Harley's old red pick-up truck. The goose was in Elfy's arms now, and Jessie was about to climb into the cab beside her, when she remembered.

"The hospital!"

Harley looked at her with alarm.

"No, it's okay. You two go ahead," she said. There was no telling how long it would take to deal with the goose. "I'll take the boat into town."

Harley's eyes searched hers, then he reached out and stroked his palm along the side of her face. As he did,

Jessie leaned towards him and kissed his full lips.

"Good luck!" Elfy mouthed, and they pulled away.

Jessie watched them drive off, a man, an old woman and a goose with a yellow sweatshirt over its head.

What a crazy start to the day, she thought as she made her way to the house. She hoped it wasn't a bad omen.

• • •

Alex ran all morning. From client to client, she forced herself to talk, the words cutting at her tender throat like pieces of glass. At times, she thought she might spit blood along with the words, but she soldiered on. Her father had taught her well: when the going got tough, the tough got going.

Now, her voice was so low and slow, she sounded like a tape player with failing batteries. When her secretary buzzed to say her mother was on the line, she took the call. If her mother was phoning, that meant she was in a manic phase, and Alex wouldn't be required to say anything anyway.

Alex tried to figure out how many years her mother had been seeing Dr. Medler. The renowned psychiatrist had come to see her mother for decades. He drove up in his Mercedes every Friday at two. And charged double for the home visit, of course. At that hourly rate, what incentive was there to make her mother better? Surely after that many years of treatment, her mother should be able to venture further than the mail box at the end of the drive?

Her poor father. Once, halfway through a bottle of bourbon, he'd admitted the marriage had been a mistake.

"But it didn't turn out all bad," Angus had told her, his eyes as shiny as the ice in his scotch. "I got you out of it. The best son-daughter a guy ever had."

The "son-daughter" thing was a private joke arising out of a time when Alex, aged seven, had told her father she wanted to be just like him when she grew up.

"You can't be *exactly* like me," he'd said. "When you grow up, you'll be a woman."

"I'll look like a woman," little Alex had conceded. "But I'll *act* like a man."

Thus, her son-daughtership began. Angus had taught her everything he knew as he paid her way through a prestigious law school. She didn't really need a law degree to be in the firm, but he'd thought it would be helpful. Money and the law went hand in hand, he always said. And money was important to her father. Although she'd never said it to him, she thought it was because of her mother's ample financial resources that he hadn't filed for divorce. She could hardly blame him. He deserved something for all the dysfunction he'd had to put up with.

Alex arranged the phone in the crook between her ear and shoulder as her mother droned on about her health. She flipped through the mail, forgetting to keep her eye out for anything bulky. Opening a small box, a dead bird fell into her lap.

Her hands froze in mid air. For a moment, she sat perfectly still and simply stared at it. Was it a canary? Forcing herself to move, she said goodbye to her mother, leaned forward and pulled a tissue from the box on her desk. Not wanting to touch the bird, she wrapped the tissue around one of its wiry legs, lifted it up and dropped it into the wastebasket.

The Bird Man, as she'd come to call him, had struck again. It had been weeks since he'd sent anything. Why did he have to send birds? Dead worms or frogs she could have coped with. She debated whether or not to call the police. If she did, she knew they'd ask her if she knew who the Bird Man was. Would she tell them? Did she know? The man whom she suspected had come to her for financial advice about a year ago, stressing from the onset that he wanted his portfolio to have "environmental integrity". As usual, she'd been busy, so she'd tossed his money into standard investments to buy herself some time, then promptly forgot. A while later, he'd stormed into her office, furious about having stock in a company logging the rainforest.

While he stood in front of her, shaking with anger, she did a quick tabulation of his profits and thrust the figures into his hands. Money had a way of smoothing things over. Unfortunately, the sum she'd written had only incensed him more, and he'd ripped the paper up and thrown the pieces at her. A week later, a dead bird had come in the mail. That was the day she'd had her first anxiety attack. The attacks had come frequently after that, making her heart palpitate and her palms sweat. When she had gone to her doctor for medication, he'd suggested she see a psychiatrist, so she'd changed doctors. There was no way she was going to a shrink. There was nothing wrong with *her* head.

If only the corpses hadn't been birds. She loved birds. One of her few happy memories as a child had been sitting in the back garden watching the birds take off and land. She must have been about five then and had wanted desperately to fly. She and her mother had even cut wings out of cardboard and strapped them to Alex's arms with masking tape. When Alex sprained her ankle jumping off the back fence, her father had found out and forbidden further attempts. He told her if she wanted to be airborne, he'd take her up in a plane.

Desperate to get her mind off the dead bird, she pulled out a motivational tape. *Success in Sixty Minutes,* the box said. That should get her back in the swing of things. She put her feet on the desk and pushed her chair back.

"Nothing to do, princess?"

Her father's boyish, muscular body filled the doorway.

"Angus!"

He winked and grinned. "Come for a drink," he said. "Let's see if we can blast that fog horn out of your throat with some Chivas."

Alex smiled and stood up. Her mother hadn't even noticed her voice. At Blue Beard's, he ordered drinks, then offered her a slim cigar and lit it.

"The Raynors are looking forward to meeting you." He took a slug of his drink. "I didn't even try rearranging." His eyes narrowed. "I know it's a sacrifice giving up Christina's thing…"

"Pageant!"

She had to shout the word to get it out. She noticed the assumption he was making and frowned. The pageant was the last event of the school year, and Alex had promised she'd be there, if only to make up for the other events she'd missed. She undid her jacket. Why was it so hot in here?

"I had to miss things when you were growing up," he said. "You understood."

Had she?

He squeezed her arm as if to press the truth of this more firmly into her body. She sipped her Bloody Mary.

The tomato juice was so thick she could hardly swallow it.

"You're the only man-woman for the job." He grinned again.

Alex was having difficulty keeping her head up. She felt like a puppet with a frayed string. The smoke was getting to her, and she began to cough. When an associate came over to talk to her father, she took the opportunity to slip away. She felt worse than she'd ever felt in her life.

Back on the eighteenth floor, where Lockhart and Lockhart had their sumptuous headquarters, Mrs. M. was pushing the coffee trolley.

"Lord in heaven, what's matter?"

Alex had known the rotund Italian woman for years. She wanted to tell her how wretched she felt, but words were beyond her now. Mrs. M. reached forward and put her hand on Alex's forehead. Her full chest came close to Alex's face.

"Hot. You need go home."

Woozily, Alex stared into Mrs. M.'s moon-round, worried face, then looked down at the woman's ample breasts. All she wanted was to lay her head on their swelling motherliness. Shocked at herself, she lifted her hand to wave away Mrs. M.'s concerns, but something was wrong.

As if her arm were a magic wand, the filing cabinets jumped into the air.

The desks rose up too, and she felt herself dropping through the air like a shot bird. Then, something hit her. It had carpet on it, just like the floor.

Chapter 3

Dressed and ready to go, Jessie put her knapsack in the boat and checked her watch. Why had she thought she was so short of time? She still had half an hour before she had to leave for the station. She considered driving the boat over to Maggie's to see how everyone was doing, but knew it wasn't a good idea. The incident with the goose had her agitated enough. She felt as if she'd jumped up on a roof and couldn't get down.

Thinking that meditation might calm her, she sat cross-legged on the dock. Closing her eyes, she brought her attention to her breath and began to pull the air in and out of her lungs. The rise and fall of her breathing soothed her. At the beginning, thoughts kept jostling her focus, but she used the rhythm of her breathing to anchor her until an easy stillness began to seep through her body and mind.

As she felt herself "land", she became aware of the warmth of the wood on the dock and the slight whiffle of breeze moving across her face from the lake. She smiled. Both the warmth of the wood and the breeze had been there when she first sat down, but she hadn't been occupying her physical senses enough to notice them. It was amazing to her. The world was such an incredibly pleasurable place, full of sensual delights she missed most of the time, because she was in her head rather than in her body. Then, realizing these were thoughts too, she brought her attention back to her breath and entered the stillness again.

The sound of the jet-ski shattered the quietness like a brick through glass. Her eyes bolted open. It was that kid on the jet-ski again! DJ! The noise blasted into her. Never had she hated a sound as much as she hated the sound of a jet-ski. The noise was worse than a snow machine, worse than a chain saw, worse than anything.

Lifting the binoculars, she scanned the lake until the jet-ski loomed in front of her, huge in the magnified lenses. The boat was shaped like a ski-doo, or snow machine, except it had no skis on the front and was about half the size of a regular fiberglass boat. This one had magenta flames painted on its sides and a slash of purple down the centre. The boy straddling the seat looked about seventeen and had rubbery-white skin. Spikes of orange hair darted out of his head like nails.

The boy gashed the water, then gashed it again, turning one way, then another, churning up the smooth surface of the lake. In her day, boats were made of fine woods, had deep-throated engines and arched prows that cut through the water with elegant swiftness. They had class. The jet-ski was like a brash piece of Tupperware.

DJ began gunning the boat, making it buck up and out of the water, then let it slap back down on the surface of the lake.

Whack. Whack. Whack.

Was he going to do that all morning? Didn't he care about the gas he was spewing into the lake? Or the peace and quiet he was wrecking? Then she thought about the goose. Was Elfy right? Had DJ been the one to shoot it down? Suddenly, she felt hot and prickly. Calm down, she told herself. Calm down.

She forced herself to breathe again, and in a moment the sound of the boat receded. Good, she thought. Then she heard birds squawking. She opened her eyes and saw DJ gunning his boat toward Bird Island. She stood up, jumped in the tin boat and pulled the cord on the old eighteen-horsepower engine.

On her way out to him, she tried to rein in her fury. If she came on too strong, she'd just get the kid's back up. And if he was as volatile as she'd been told, that would be counterproductive. Besides, she shouldn't jump to conclusions. Maybe no one had told the kid about the bird sanctuary. She'd give him the facts, keep her cool and try to suss him out about the goose.

When she was close to him, she waved, but he kept gouging the water with his boat. Didn't he see her? Of course he saw her! He was ignoring her, the little creep! Then he was racing around her. Round and round and she began to feel dizzy. Rage jolted her up and she stood and shook her fists at him. He slowed his boat to an idle. The garbling sound of the engine pulverized her thoughts and she wanted to put her hands over her ears and shut her eyes. She pointed to the island. "That's a sanctuary there. Birds are nesting!"

The boy stared at her, his face sullen. Up close, he seemed so young. His youth softened her. She'd try a different tack, tell him—

"Fuck you," he said, gunned the boat and was gone.

Jessie reeled back as if she'd been slapped. She couldn't believe what she'd heard.

Fuck you. Fuck you. Fuck you.

The words kept firing at her over and over again. Feeling bruised and beaten, she started the engine again. Now, *there* was someone who needed to be taught a lesson. With a deep sense of foreboding, she steered her boat into the bay and headed home.

• • •

In the hospital bed, Alex twisted and turned. In her fevered dream, flames singed her legs and scorched her clothes. She could smell the stench of them burning. Despite the pain in her throat, she tried to shout, to tell whoever was out there that she wasn't who they thought, but there was no one listening. Then her father appeared and told her to get back to work. He didn't seem to understand that any moment now, she was going to burst like a roasting sausage.

Faces appeared, inches away. Tom, the children, women in strange white caps who made her swallow things. After she swallowed, the heat went away, then came back worse than ever. Her flesh was on fire. Her skin bubbled. All she knew of herself was going up in flames. Somewhere, someone was whimpering. It sounded very far away. It sounded like someone she used to be.

• • •

Near the back, between the railway cars, Jessie found a place to stick her head outside. The wind hit her head hard, yanking her hair back, but she didn't mind. She imagined the wind streaming through her mind, sweeping DJ's words away. For hours now, they'd been repeating, and she wanted to be free of them. For once, she was glad to be going to the city. She wanted to be as far away from the boy and his boat as possible.

Forcing her eyes open, she looked ahead and saw a jumble of huge boxes scattered across the landscape. Toronto. There was a grey-purple bruise of cloud over the city, and the air began to smell like the dump. Earlier, in her seat, the man next to her had been listening to a radio and she'd heard the announcer warning people with chest conditions to stay indoors. Stay indoors? What if you had a job? Kids? It was an outrage that people had to put up with smog like this. Someday, someone was going to launch a legal suit against a city for letting the air stink like this. Having clean air should be a fundamental human right!

When the train pulled into Toronto, she hefted her knapsack to her back and walked through the station. It was like a giant snail shell, made out of glass. Once she was through the revolving doors, she looked up. Black towers, mirrored towers, needle-nosed towers rose above her, sixty, seventy, eighty stories high. Their compressed density pushed down on her and for a second, she wanted to run back inside. Then, hearing some sparrows, she caught a glimpse of them in a small maple tree across from the station and stepped forward. If they could make a life in such a metropolis, she could make a visit.

"Shit, lady!" Someone bumped her from behind.

Rule #1 in the city: keep moving. Despite the pain in her foot, she increased her speed and tried not to gawk as she knew people from small towns were prone to do.

No one looked at her. And why should they? This wasn't a small town where you were likely to run into someone you knew. Or might know. She smiled, remembering how she used to honk at slow drivers when she'd first moved to Muskoka. Honked until one day, late for an appointment for a mortgage, she'd blasted a red-headed woman for not moving when the light turned green. She had met the woman again a few minutes later behind a sign that said "mortgages". The woman had not been smiling.

Although she liked the relatedness of people in a small town, she didn't like the lack of cultural diversity. Here, in the throng of people passing her by, was a man with pink hair skating along on roller blades, two women in saris with red dots on their foreheads, a kid in a muscle shirt that had a big finger on the front, an Asian girl carrying a violin case—the variety was endless.

Jessie scanned their faces. Were these people happy? Were they leading lives that felt meaningful to them? It was something she always asked new clients: "Are you on course with your life?" It was amazing how few said "yes".

For some, a life purpose shone like a flashlight, illuminating every step of the way. Her client, Bill, for example, had spent hours as a child drawing and now had paintings in galleries all over the world. For most people, however, finding their true path wasn't so easy. She thought about the flock of geese she'd seen that morning and their incredible ability to navigate across thousands of miles to find their way home. They were lucky; they had some sort of inner homing device that told them when they were on their true path.

Jessie liked to think of psychotherapy as a homing device too. Like many counsellors, she imagined herself as a kind of psychological compass, helping people find their way back to the truth about themselves. Which, depending on how far from home they'd roamed, could take a little or a lot of time. And sometimes, as with the goose that had been shot down, a few repairs were necessary before they were up and running.

What amazed Jessie in the relationship between the person and their path was the way the path itself called out. She'd seen it over and over again in her work. One of her clients would be searching for their "true north" or the right way to go, and meanwhile, that very path was talking to them, whispering through dreams and symptoms and life events—*this way, no, not that way! Over here!* The lines from a poem came to her.

"Meanwhile, the wild geese high in the clear blue air are heading home again. Whoever you are, no matter how lonely, the world offers itself to you, calls to you like the wild geese, harsh and exciting, over and over again, announcing your place..."

Announcing your place. Your place. And how did you know where your place was? Her clients were always asking her this.

"Because when you find your place, you start to thrive," she told them. Like a daisy thrives in the sun or a violet in the dappled woods.

Seeing the hospital up ahead, she crossed the street at the lights. This stint in the hospital would be her first time away from work in years. Usually she was as healthy as the day was long, but over the last while, her foot had become more of a problem. Her work had taught her to pay attention to the messages of the body. The pain in Don's shoulders told him he was "shouldering" too much weight. Tina's sore throats came every time she stopped herself from speaking out to her boss.

Her doctor scoffed at her when she talked like this. He

called this kind of thinking reductionist and argued that the pain in her foot, for example, had to do with tendons and nothing more. She, however, wasn't so willing to ignore the psychological component of symptoms. To her, the mind-body connection was real—as anyone who'd had a sexual fantasy knew.

So, what was her foot saying? Feet had to do with going forward. Was she heading in the wrong direction? She was loath to even consider this. Not after all the work she'd done on her Ph.D. She only had four courses left. This was no time for doubts. But, if she had doubts, shouldn't she face them? Not now. She didn't want to think about it now.

In front of the hospital was a line of ash trees set in concrete boxes. She stood beside one of the trees. It wasn't happy. She could tell. Its leaves were grimy, and the whole tree had a limpness to it. For a moment, she had an intense yearning for home, but made herself climb the steps and enter the huge chrome and glass revolving doors. Inside the building, the animal of her body tensed. She could almost feel the fear and pain clawing at the air. Now she wished she'd let Harley come.

Following the sign, she went to Admitting and was met by a plump nurse with a brown wart on her nostril. Jessie filled out the forms the woman handed her. Dearborn-James, Jessie. Five-foot five. Hundred and forty pounds. Hair, blond, silver, grey? She wrote in all three. No, she'd never had tuberculosis and didn't have AIDS. There should be a category called "healthy". She smiled. There she went, trying to change things again. When she was done, she handed the papers back.

The nurse snapped a plastic band around Jessie's wrist. "We've got you now!"

Chapter 4

The stiff sheets smelled of bleach, and Jessie felt as if she'd slept in a cardboard envelope. There were no sweet smells of night-cleansed air here, no rousing first-light chorus of birdsong. Her mouth cracked with dryness. She yearned for water but knew she couldn't have any until after the surgery. Her stomach felt like a gymnasium full of kids doing back flips.

"Fear is a big horse," Harley once told her. "Learn to ride it and you can go anywhere."

Dear Harley. He was right. Fear was a big horse. This morning it felt like a bucking bronco. What she would give to have his arms around her for a moment. Then, remembering their "date", she slipped down into the warmth of the bed and went to him.

They had agreed to do this, to be together at dawn, so she envisioned where he'd be, sitting by the wide-girthed pine tree near the lake. Even in her imagination, she was warmed by the sight of him. She took his hand. It was so real, so strong to her senses, she was only dimly aware of an orderly coming for her, only vaguely cognizant of gliding along a corridor, the "ping" of an elevator, the sound of doors, then the sharp prick of a needle. Ten, nine, eight, four, seven...

• • •

In the heat, many hands came. Alex could feel them on her body, probing and jabbing. These hands were cool and unfamiliar. They intruded themselves upon her, and she had no energy to withstand their invasions. Alex didn't like these hands.

Sometimes she could feel Tom's hands. They were gentle. They stroked her forehead, pulled covers to her throat, but they were worried hands, and she didn't want their worry. A few times in the night, another pair of hands came. She had never known hands like these. What they did wasn't so different from the other hands, they gave her water, put compresses on her forehead, but they were so peaceful. She felt as if she could drink their calmness. Who did they belong to? Sometimes she looked up, but in her fever, all was blurry.

• • •

Even through the muzzle of drugs, Jessie's foot howled with pain. She knew she could take more medication, but it made her woozy, so she tried to distract herself by listening to her roommates. They had all introduced themselves yesterday. Unfortunately, Alex, the woman with pneumonia who was across from her, hadn't stopped pontificating since she'd come out of her fever. Lucy, the other woman, was listening with rapt attention. Jessie was grateful they were talking. As long as these two were socializing, she didn't have to.

Through partially closed eyes, Jessie observed Alex. Even from her bed she could see Alex's plucked eyebrows and moisturized skin—all the trappings of an affluent, cosmopolitan lifestyle. You'd think financial success would allow people to relax, Jessie mused. But it wasn't so. Too often, getting the good things involved having to push until that's all a person knew how to do. Alex struck her as the kind of woman who had done a lot of pushing. And a lot of controlling. Was she always this way? Probably not, Jessie thought. In her experience, traumatic situations usually made a person's defence mechanisms worse. To someone with control patterns, like Alex, being in the hospital where other people called the shots would be like a strip search.

"You work *where*, Lucy?" Alex was asking. It was more of a demand than a question.

"At a bank—"

"A bank! You'll never get anywhere in a bank!"

"I—it was all…"

"Investigate investment companies. That's where the money is!"

Let the woman finish a sentence, for goodness sake, Jessie muttered to herself. And you, Lucy, stand up for yourself. She looked over at the woman in the bed beside her. Lucy wasn't much more than a teenager. No wonder she was intimidated by Alex. As well as being a bulldozer, Alex was old enough to be Lucy's mother. In fact, Alex looked like she could even be Lucy's mother, the resemblance was so striking.

The orderly came in with lunch. Jessie sat up and fingered a greasy triangle of grilled cheese sandwich. Processed cheese on white bread. How could anyone get well on this kind of food? She nibbled the coleslaw.

"I should know," Alex said. "I *own* an investment company."

"You own one? Wow." Lucy looked over at Jessie to see if she was impressed too. Jessie kept her face neutral. She'd had years of practice.

Alex turned to Jessie. "What do you do?"

"I work as a psychotherapist." Jessie saw Alex cringe ever so slightly.

"You kind of look familiar," Lucy said. "Are you famous or something?"

Jessie laughed. "No."

Alex kept interrogating. "You work in the city?"

"The city? You mean Toronto?" Jessie chuckled. "No. I'm from up north. Muskoka. I have a little place in the woods." She could see the interest fall out of Alex's eyes. There it was. The urban chauvinism she detested. It was all right to cottage in Muskoka, that had class, but to actually *live* north of Barrie, that made you a country bumpkin for sure.

"You live in the woods?" Lucy asked. "Aren't you afraid of something happening?"

Jessie smiled. "Like what? A police chase through the trees? A gang of skinheads stealing my garden tools?" It amused her how dangerous city people sometimes thought the country was.

"What about bears?" Lucy said. "I was at my aunt's place in Muskoka two summers ago and this bear smashed her gazebo."

"Bears get hungry, just like people," Jessie said. "And if you leave food out, they'll go for it. Even if it's inside a gazebo. Private property isn't something they understand."

Alex rolled her eyes at Lucy. "Listen to her defend the bear."

Jessie corralled her irritation and looked outside. A

group of pigeons was cooing on her window sill. Oh, to be a bird and be able to fly off whenever you wanted.

On an impulse, Jessie picked up the phone and tried Harley again. Yesterday when she'd talked to him, he'd had some disturbing news.

"There's a rumour flying around that Dick Price paid some architect four grand," he'd told her.

"Four grand! What for?" A person didn't pay four grand to design a laundry room."

"That's the big question," Harley said.

"Sounds like an expansion."

"And smells like skunk."

"I thought you liked skunks."

"I do, but…"

"DJ out there today?" She wanted to ask, but wouldn't let herself. She needed to calm down about the boy and knew she wouldn't if she kept talking about him.

"Harley, what's that sound?"

"What sound?"

"That whistle."

"A bird. Hey, know what? Charlie hasn't wagged his tail since you left. Neither have I."

"Don't worry," she said. "I'll wag yours as soon as I get home."

"Good. Meanwhile, I'm going to find out about those architect fees."

"Let me know."

But he hadn't let her know. And now no one was answering. When her own voice came on and explained why no one could come to the phone, she hung up. Alex was still holding forth. This time she was expounding the virtues of a global economy.

"Think of it," Alex was saying. "As the third world becomes richer, they'll want all the technological advances the West has. The phones, computers, microwaves. Think of the boom for the automotive industry when people in India can afford cars."

Jessie couldn't hold herself back. "And think of the pollution. The ozone layer can't handle the emissions we have now."

Alex looked at her like she was speaking Swahili, then returned her gaze to Lucy and carried on.

"The point is, in a market economy, opportunities are everywhere. That's why you have to get yourself out there."

"But I—"

"Don't say, 'but'. You've got to go *after* an employer, *convince* him to hire you."

As Jessie listened, she tried to guess the kind of family Alex must have come from. She imagined a strong, overbearing father; that would create a psyche ripe for domination by the masculine. But she'd bet the father wasn't as stable as he pretended. Stable men didn't need to yank the feminine out by the roots as someone had obviously done with Alex. And the mother? The mother would have to be weak, too weak to stop the father from driving the girl from the open-armed feminine strengths of intuition and receptivity into the tempting security of closed-fisted control.

What would it take to change someone like Alex? Getting away from her father would be a start, Jessie thought, but in her experience, overbearing fathers usually kept their children on tight psychological leashes. Hadn't she heard Alex saying something yesterday about working with her dad? That fit the picture. It would take a hefty jolt to unlock a pattern as firmly entrenched as that. A few years of therapy might do it, but Alex didn't strike her as the kind of person who would do therapy. Even if she did, with control patterns like hers, she'd fight her therapist every step of the way.

But who knows, Jessie thought. Maybe being sick would give Alex a chance to listen to herself more deeply. Get under that armoured persona and see what was there. Illness had a way of providing such an opportunity, and in that way, it was good. It created a pit-stop for those necessary realignments to take place. And if she did realign, Alex's health would only benefit. When the mind and body were squabbling, even if only subconsciously, a lot of energy was lost.

Yes, illness had a way of bringing a person to their psychological knees. Illness and the fear it generated. Love and fear—they were the great transformers. Jessie had seen so many clients careening down the highway of life, their souls racing after them, shouting futile messages into the exhaust fumes. Then they fell in love or got sick, and they were suddenly thrown off track into the wilderness. At that moment, their souls could catch up. When they did, they often spoke with life-changing clarity.

Alex's voice broke into her reverie. Now she was advising Lucy. "You've got to take control of your life."

Jessie sighed. That's right, yank your life behind you like an unwilling dog and teach Lucy how to do the same. Great.

"When I get back to Lockhart and Lockhart, I'll see if there's anything—"

"Would you? Would you really?"

How perfect these two were for each other, Jessie

thought. Alex was desperate to be in the know, and Lucy was desperate to have someone know. Alex needed to give advice, and Lucy needed to get advice. Their patterns meshed completely. And even though it looked as if Lucy needed Alex more than the other way around, Jessie knew this wasn't true. In fact, it would probably shock Alex to realize how much she needed Lucy. But, unless fate turned the tables, she probably wouldn't ever find out.

Strange, Jessie thought, how different a person could look on the outside from the way they really were on the inside. New clients reminded her of this all the time. People would come in and present themselves in a certain way, but as Jessie often found out, that persona wasn't always congruent with what was going on at a deeper level. It wasn't that people lied. It was just that they'd learned to put a mask on to get by in the world.

Jessie didn't know Alex but sensed that beneath the woman's confident, almost overbearing exterior, there was a quieter, softer soul. Which made sense. Why else would a person have as hard an exterior as Alex if there wasn't something soft and mushy that needed protecting?

Jessie sighed. Thinking like this made her feel like she was back at work. Feeling restless, she picked up the little book of poems she'd brought. Over the years, she'd copied all her favourites into a small hard-covered book. Now, not only did she have them in one place, but she could easily take them with her: Blake, Mary Oliver, Dylan Thomas, Kathleen Rain, Rilke.

Sometimes she read poems to clients. Poems had a way of zigzagging through a person's defences and finding the target of truth faster than any wisdom she might utter. If she selected the right poem, she could almost feel the person's spirit coming out to feed on it. And once the spirit was involved, the healing could begin.

She flipped through the poems and her eyes fell on the lines from a poem by Yeats. "*And I will arise and go now, and go to Innisfree, and a small cabin build there of clay and wattles made...*"

The chatter in the room receded. "*And I shall have some peace there for peace comes dropping slow...*" A lovely, relaxed feeling came over her. "*I hear lake water lapping with low sounds by the shore...*" She closed her eyes and imagined herself on the dock with Harley. "*While standing on the roadway or on the pavements grey I hear it in my deep heart's core...*"

The sound of lake water washed over her and she was about to sink into the abyss of sleep when Lucy's voice pulled her back. "I've got it! You're that tree lady!"

Jessie opened her eyes and tried to read Lucy's face to see whether this was a good thing to admit to or not.

"That's why you looked familiar. My aunt has a picture of you on her fridge. You know, the one that was in the paper, the one of you chained to the tree...Wow! You *are* famous." Lucy turned to Alex. "This woman saved a whole bunch of old trees." She turned back to Jessie. "You're gutsy."

It hadn't felt gutsy, Jessie wanted to say. Her body had just done it. Like her body would have stepped in front of someone trying to attack an old person. She looked over at Alex.

Gutsy or stupid, Alex's eyes said.

•   •   •

Alex lay listening to the growl of traffic. All her colleagues, anyone who was anyone, were cruising those expressways on their way to work. She yearned to be out there with them, her fingers drumming on the steering wheel, lungs pulling in the buzz of that first cigarette. She turned away from the window, feeling like a damaged cog.

If she didn't get out of here soon, she was going to go crazy. She closed her eyes. *Get a grip.* She tried to settle herself down, but couldn't. She wished she could bring those hands back, feel them stroking her forehead again, but she couldn't conjure them up. They had disappeared along with her fever. She'd remembered her kids having hallucinations like that when they were ill.

She looked over to see if Lucy was still sleeping. The girl reminded her so much of Christina. Before Christina had turned into a bleached Bob Marley. She felt such a fondness for the girl. And Lucy seemed enamoured with her too, just like Christina had been once upon a time. Last evening, for example, when Lucy had seen Alex struggling to get up, she'd offered to go and get her the evening paper. When was the last time either of her children had offered to do anything like that?

At the moment, Lucy was paying her more attention than her father, for God's sake. Why hadn't he visited? She frowned at the store full of flowers on her windowsill. Tom came to see her every day, often bringing Evan, or sometimes Christina. Even Mrs. M. had stopped by. But not her father. *What was she, a trained seal, valued only when performing?* The thought shocked her. The orderly brought breakfast, and she sat up. A yellow eye stared back at her. It smelled of cheap fat. She pushed the plate away and stared at her two roommates. "I *hate* this. I *hate* being sick. I can't just keep missing work. I've got clients who count on me, people—"

Jessie looked over at her. "Enjoy it. When you're old and on your death bed, you won't wish you spent more time working."

"Oh, yes, I will," Alex retorted. Her work was extremely important to her. She turned to Lucy. "Where'd you get that paper last night?"

Lucy pulled herself out of bed and put on her housecoat. "Would you like me to get it for you?"

Alex nodded. Christina should be here to see this.

"Lucy, you look pale," Jessie said." Are you sure you should be moving around?"

"I'm fine." Lucy looked at Alex uncertainly.

Alex gave a slight nod to Lucy and was pleased when the girl carried on. She could use someone with that kind of attitude at the office.

"She looked perfectly fine to me," Alex said, glaring at Jessie. Jessie did not look away. In fact, Jessie seemed to look right into her. Alex picked up the stiff envelope of documents she'd had Sue, her secretary, courier over. Feeling like an addict about to get a hit, she opened it with relish and scanned one of the pages. Then she scanned it again. Maybe it was the drugs, or maybe it was the fact that she hadn't used her brain for days, but she couldn't concentrate. The figures were like a bunch of hieroglyphics she didn't know how to interpret.

Frightened, she pushed the file aside. She just needed some coffee, that's all. She'd try again in a few minutes. Just then Lucy came back with the paper. Alex reached in her purse and pressed some coins into Lucy's palm. The girl's hand was deathly cold.

• • •

The doctor entered the room and stopped at Jessie's bed, instructing the nurse to undo her foot bandages.

"Amazing how they teach nurses how to do bandages and not doctors," Jessie said.

A dark look came over the doctor's face. The nurse smiled but didn't look up. Don't, Jessie said to herself. She knew she shouldn't goad him. No matter how bad a mood she was in. Not if she wanted to get out of here. Which she did. With things so unsettled at home, she hated being away. It was just that this doctor had the attitude of a despot. Talk about control issues. This guy must have been at the top of his class in Introductory Arrogance.

There was a commotion in the hall.

"We *know* it's not visiting hours," someone said in a loud voice.

Jessie looked towards the door. She recognized those voices.

Elfy strode in. "We're not staying." She bent to kiss Jessie, then moved out of the way so a large-chested, authoritative woman could greet Jessie as well.

"Aggie," Jessie said.

The doctor opened his mouth to speak, but Aggie put her ringed hand in his. "Excellent facility you have here, doctor. I'm on the board of South Muskoka Hospital."

The doctor closed his mouth. Elfy looked down at the foot the nurse was unbandaging. "Thought it was the right foot…"

A crevice of doubt appeared on the doctor's face.

Elfy's eyebrows bounced to the top of her forehead as if they were hitting a celebratory bell. "Just kidding, doc—"

She winked at Jessie and grinned. "You can never, always, sometimes tell." The old woman had gotten him and gotten him good. To his credit, however, he seemed to be taking it well. Although he'd returned his attention to her foot, there was a wry curl on his lips.

"They treating you right?" Elfy asked Jessie.

"I *told* her it wasn't visiting hours," Aggie said.

"We're just down buying cages. I mean corsets. You know Aggie, she needs those special sizes." Elfy held her arms out as if she were holding two huge beach balls.

Aggie elbowed Elfy and looked at Jessie. "Harley's coming to get you tomorrow."

Jessie saw the doctor's eyebrows furrow. *Herr Doktor* was obviously displeased he hadn't been consulted. But, the one good thing about control freaks was that they were easy to please. All you had to do was offer them some control. She turned to Aggie. "Only if the doctor thinks I'm ready." The doctor's eyebrows unfurrowed. She suppressed a smile.

Aggie tugged at Elfy's arm, blew Jessie a kiss and led Elfy out of the room.

"Nice meeting everyone," Elfy called behind to Alex.

"Yes, tomorrow you can go," the doctor said to Jessie in the sudden quiet.

●   ●   ●

Behind her Fortune 500 magazine, Alex watched Jessie pack her knapsack. Knapsack. Teenagers had knapsacks, not adults. She felt miffed that Jessie was being allowed to go home and she wasn't. It was as if Jessie were beating her at something. Well, she didn't care what the doctor said.

Whether her X-ray was clear or not, she was going home tomorrow.

As soon as she was back at work, she was going to figure out a way to hire Lucy as her personal assistant. It surprised her how attached she felt to the girl. She liked the way Lucy was always asking for advice. It made her feel motherly. And it was good to have her motherliness appreciated. Unlike Christina, who gave her the emotional finger every time Alex tried to parent her. She'd have to show Lucy off to Christina. Let her daughter see someone showing her the respect she deserved.

The only problem with hiring Lucy might be the girl's medical problem. Which was what? All Alex knew was that it had something to do with Lucy's heart. But the girl didn't look sick, didn't look sick at all. That Jessie was such a worrywart.

Should she discuss hiring Lucy with her father before mentioning it to Lucy? Normally, she would have, but she was too upset with him. Why hadn't he been in? Sure, he called every day, but he was always in such a hurry. She was lucky if he gave her two minutes of his time. Of course, part of that was because of her. He had to do *her* work as well as his. But still, couldn't he have found one hour to come and see her?

Alex watched as Jessie set the packed knapsack on the bed and waited. Some man named Harley was coming to pick her up. What a ridiculous name, she thought. He sounded like a motorcycle. She was wondering what a man named Harley might look like when Lucy handed her a piece of paper, then did the same with Jessie.

"Let's exchange addresses," Lucy said.

Alex nodded. She couldn't imagine being in touch

with Jessie again, but she put her address on two pieces of paper anyway.

"That's beautiful," Lucy said, noticing Jessie's ring. "It's jade, isn't it? Wow!" She looked at Alex. "You should see this ring, Alex. It's gorgeous."

Alex frowned. She didn't want to see Jessie's ring. She wanted to finish reading the article she'd started on offshore investing. She had to start getting with it again.

"It was my grandmother's," Jessie said. "Gramma Rivers."

"Gramma Rivers! What a lovely name," Lucy said. She glanced over at Alex, but Alex had her head back in the magazine.

"She loved rivers, too. Lived by one and died by one."

"Died by one?" Lucy asked. "How?"

"Now, there was an interesting death."

"Tell me!"

Alex frowned. She felt edgy. Death was not a topic for hospital conversation. What was it with these psychotherapists? Was no topic ever out of bounds? She cast a warning look at Lucy but couldn't get the girl's attention. Alex returned to her article, but her palms began to sweat.

"As I said," Jessie carried on, "my grandmother loved rivers. She lived by one in Scotland. And, one day, when she was eighty-two, she was sitting on a rock beside it when a huge flood of water came down the river."

"Wow! How come?"

"No one knows. But the flood of water washed her away."

Lucy raised her small hands to her mouth. "No!"

"It's the absolute truth," Jessie said. "She floated for

miles before they found her body. It was as if the river came for her."

Alex snorted. What a bunch of bunk!

"If you loved rivers, that would be a good way to die, wouldn't it?" Jessie said.

There was no such thing as a good way to die, Alex hissed under her breath.

"I guess when your number's up, your number's up," Lucy said. "And if I had to go, I'd rather go fast like that." She snapped her fingers.

Alex looked up. She wanted to stop this talk and stop it now, but saw Jessie grinning towards the door. Alex followed Jessie's eyes and saw a large man move quietly into the room and go to Jessie. Harley, she presumed. She watched them hug, and as Harley leaned forward, saw a tail of glossy hair disappear under his collar. Was the man an Indian?

As if feeling her stare, Harley turned purposefully toward Alex, his eyes steady on hers. She looked into his dark, open eyes, then pulled hers away.

In a swift, silent gesture, Harley picked up Jessie's bag and went out.

"Be right down," Jessie called after him and stopped at Lucy's bed. The two women clasped hands.

"Your hands are so cold," Jessie said, rubbing them in her own.

"Yours are like heaters," Lucy said. "Can I keep them?"

Laughing, Jessie leaned forward and gave Lucy a warm hug.

Alex tensed. She wasn't a hugger and had no intention of becoming one now. When Jessie came towards her, Alex thrust out her hand. If a handshake was enough to close a million-dollar deal, it was sufficient for a situation like this. Jessie took Alex's hand between the two of hers.

A bizarre pattern appeared in Alex's mind, reminding her of what had appeared on her computer screen when Christina had spilled hot chocolate on the keyboard once. Although she couldn't see how it was possible, Jessie's hands were somehow familiar. She was scrambling around her brain for how this could be, when a new thought broke into her mind. Were these the hands that had come to her in the night? The hands she'd attributed to her fever? As she watched Jessie walk away, she realized they were.

Chapter 5

H ome." Harley pulled the car to a stop.
Gratitude washed over Jessie. She looked at her little wooden house with the deck facing the lake. "I think I appreciate this, then I go away and appreciate it even more."

Harley frowned. "No slot machines."

On the way back, they'd stopped at the reservation and spent the night. The Native community was embroiled in discussions about whether to allow a multi-million dollar casino on the reserve, and a special meeting had been held.

"They going to go for it, you think?" Jessie asked.

Harley sat motionless. The more upset he was, the more still his body became.

"Pretty tempting, that amount of money," Jessie said, thinking of the social programs the reservation would be able to establish, programs the natives needed badly. "But the thought of hundreds of people pumping slot machines—"

"Metal masturbation."

Jessie smiled wryly. He had that right.

"There'll be no more stars," Harley said.

She nodded. The casino would be lit up like a spotlight display which would make it impossible to see the night sky. Harley had a particular fondness for night skies.

Harley got out of the car and helped her along the pathway. She turned towards the house, but Harley suddenly lifted her up and took her down to the dock, where he eased her into the wooden deck chair. Jessie sucked in a lungful of air. There was something about air near a lake that made it different from other air. It was moist and full of a soft kind of magic, as if a fish has just jumped through it, or might.

There were purple-grey clouds forming to the south. "Storm," Harley said.

Jessie listened. In the distance, she could hear rumbling. On the way home, the car radio had said the city was getting it full blast. She smiled. She liked storms. In the summer they were so intense and cleansing. Besides, if it was raining, there would be no boats on the lake. No DJ to contend with. Her stomach began to bubble as she thought about her run-in with the boy. *Fuck off. Fuck off.* The words came at her like gunfire.

Hearing a whistle, Jessie turned and saw Elfy coming down the steps with Charlie.

"Looks like you have a soccer ball instead of a foot," Elfy said. "Now you'll *really* be able to kick people."

"Yeah, should I try it out on you?" Jessie swung her foot playfully.

"Pfft." Elfy swatted the air.

Jessie turned back to look at the lake. "How's the goose?"

"We let it go yesterday." Elfy said. Harley made a chirping bird sound, and Elfy pressed her thin lips together, but her chest still bobbed up and down.

"All right, you two. What's so funny?"

Harley cawed like a raven.

"Something to do with birds?" Jessie looked at Elfy. The old woman's eyes were full of mirth.

"Should we fess up?" Elfy said to Harley.

"*We?*"

Elfy stuck her tongue out at Harley. "You're the one who started it."

"One. I brought one over."

"Never said no to the others."

"Never had the chance."

"Jessie likes birds," Elfy said. "Just tell her."

When no one spoke, Jessie said, "Come on, you two, spill the beans!"

"You're gonna love the hummingbird," Elfy said. "Flew into fly paper, for crying out loud. Lost ninety percent of his feathers. Didn't know if he was going to make it."

"What's a hummingbird got to do with—"

"Want to see him?"

"Maybe later." She didn't feel like going over to Maggie's now.

"It's not far." Elfy smirked.

"The hummingbird's here? Why?"

Elfy grimaced. "Maggie's mom had a heart attack, and she had to fly out to Alberta. We're helping out."

"I can't see a problem housing a hummingbird," Jessie said. What trouble could a hummingbird be? "Who's looking after the rest of the birds?"

Harley made insistent peeping sounds.

Elfy's glance ping-ponged between Harley and Jessie. "There's some robins too. Baby ones. No bigger than cranberries."

Harley changed to chirping sounds.

"Oh, yeah, the finch. It got mauled by a cat, but it's going to be fine."

"The blue jays—"

"Harley, she's heard enough!"

"Sounds like the entire bird refuge is here," Jessie said.

"Bingo," Elfy said. "Harley figured it'd be easier not having to trek over there every five minutes." Harley rolled his eyes, but she carried on. "Those babies have to be fed like *all the time*. We didn't want to tell you when you were in the hospital, in case…"

"In case I disagreed? Since when did that stop either of you?" Jessie smiled and struggled to her feet. "Let's go have a look."

Inside the house, Jessie was greeted with a symphony of bird sounds: chirping, chittering, whistles and caws. It was like being in the middle of a forest. It made her feel airy and light just listening to it. Following the sounds, she went into the guest room and saw a series of bird cages arranged on card tables. The cages had wooden slats on the front and small doors for feeding.

Not wanting to frighten the birds by coming in too quickly, she stood in the doorway, but even from there she could make out a finch, a mallard, a yellow-bellied sapsucker, a grackle and a blue jay. Each cage contained a flash of colour. Winged beauty, that's what birds were. It was enthralling just to be in the same room with them. She leaned forward and peered into a cage of baby robins. They were so tiny! Her heart flew open like a window.

"Time to feed the babies," Elfy said as she began to mix up some mash. She filled a needleless syringe and handed it to Harley who fed the mixture to the waiting babies. The bright yellow triangles of their mouths were open wide. Their cheeping was so loud that Jessie didn't hear the phone.

"I'd better get that," Harley said. "Might be another admission." In a moment, he came back to tell Jessie the phone was for her.

"Oh, I wanted to see you feed them," Jessie said, irritated at being pulled away.

Elfy smiled at Harley. "See? She's got bird fever as bad as we do."

Thinking the call might be from one of her children, Jessie hopped into the next room and took the phone. The sound she heard made her immediately regret answering the call. The sound she heard was someone trying not to cry. In her line of work, it wasn't uncommon to get calls from upset clients, and sometimes this meant listening to them cry. She didn't mind hearing people cry. It was when people tried not to cry that she got frustrated. Because when people tried *not* to cry, they often tried to talk, which ended up with them making a lot of squeaking sounds that she could never understand. Tuning back into the caller, she listened more carefully, trying to decipher either the identity of the caller or the nature of their distress.

The only word fragment she could make out was something that sounded like "loo" or "loose". Whatever that meant. She sat down to wait it out and began to breathe. Perhaps if she were calm, it would help calm the caller as well. As she breathed and listened, she was able to pick a word from the scree: Lucy. Then it clicked who the caller was.

"Alex! Is that you? Has something happened to Lucy?"

The clarity in her voice knocked Alex into a moment of composure.

"Lucy—"

"Lucy, is something the matter with Lucy?"

"She's…she's dead."

Dead. The word hit Jessie like a rock in the belly. Pulling hard for breath, she closed her eyes and tried to calm herself.

"What?" Jessie spat the word out. It was hoarse and full of fear.

Alex's voice went squeaky again. "An em…an embo—"

"Embolism."

"This morning. I—" She took a break and made another run at the words. "I—I saw her."

"Oh, Alex." A swell of concern for Alex washed through her. Had Lucy been dead long before Alex saw her? Had rigor mortis set in? Suddenly, Jessie saw the stiff body of her husband after a massive coronary had taken him more than ten years before. She had been the one to find him. Seeing his dead body, seeing anyone's dead body, was an assault to the senses. Sudden death was so unnerving. That someone, anyone, could vibrate with life one minute and be as rigid as ice the next, was monumentally shocking. Just yesterday, she'd hugged Lucy, felt the slippery softness of her hair against her cheek.

Alex's sniffling brought her back to the moment. She wanted to cry, sob, wail. And would do all of those things later. But at the moment, Alex needed attention. Given how tightly Alex gripped life, she must feel as if her steering wheel had just turned to jelly. Hearing her trying to hold back her emotions, Jessie whispered, "Let it go, Alex, let it go." But Alex couldn't let go. She'd armoured herself for too long. People like Alex had a metal shield around them that made them almost impervious to life's onslaughts. But when they got knocked over, which they always did, the weight of their armour made it almost impossible to get up again.

"Breathe with me for a few minutes," Jessie said.

"What?"

"Breathe with me." Tension was clenching her own chest, so it wasn't easy, but Jessie closed her eyes and thought of ocean waves, rolling in and rolling out. The breath: the great primordial energy bank. It was the beginning place. Breathing was the first thing a person did when they came into the world and the last thing they did when they left. It was also the fastest way she knew to get herself or someone else back on centre.

A calm space opened up between them, and Alex spoke into it.

"I just thought I should—that you'd want to…know." She paused, took a truncated breath. "Oh, Jessie, I'm so frigh—"

"It's okay to be frightened," Jessie said. She heard Alex take a breath and waited for her to speak.

"I feel like…like I'm falling apart."

Of course, Jessie thought. When people with control patterns let go, they felt as if they were losing it. "Keep talking," she said. "I'm listening." She wanted Alex to know she was willing to help her, to stick by her as she struggled through her feelings.

There was a clicking sound on the phone.

"Alex…? Are you there?"

Had she hung up? No! Something must have gone wrong! Jessie put down the phone quickly so Alex could call back. She waited for it to ring, but it didn't. Deciding to call the hospital, she lifted the receiver. There was no dial tone. Then she remembered the storm. Lightning must have knocked a tree down somewhere south of there. Phone lines snapped like thread when a tree fell on them. She sighed. There was nothing to do but wait.

• • •

The phone sat in Alex's hand like a dead thing.

"I'm sorry, but that line is still out of service," the recorded message told her once again. She had been dialling Jessie's line every few minutes for hours now. Little blips of nervousness shot down her arms and her palms were sweating. With shaking fingers, she placed the phone back on the receiver. Was there someone else she could call? She rummaged through the possibilities, but no one felt safe enough.

An orderly entered the room, pushing an elderly woman in a wheel chair. He helped the woman into the newly made-up bed.

"NO! That's Lucy's bed," Alex wanted to scream.

Agitated, wheezy, she thrust the sheets aside. She was going to march down to the office and demand another room. Be insistent. But she didn't feel insistent. She felt weak and ill and on the verge of going out of her mind.

In a panic, she pushed herself into the hall in her hospital gown and slippers. She was the one who should have had the heart attack. She smoked, never exercised. Was it possible to bring one on? Her heart thumped erratically in her chest. Was this normal? Beside her, elevator doors opened. Inside, a nurse was standing beside a bed trolley. On the trolley was a mound covered with a sheet. The sheet had a peak near the top and another near the bottom. Alex felt the blood drain from her face. It was a corpse. The elevator doors closed, but the vision of the cadaver stayed.

Alex swallowed hard. Hurrying to her room, she stepped into her shoes, pulled on some slacks under her gown and headed down the back stairs. When she was on the main floor, she tucked her nightgown in, added a sweater and slipped out the side door.

When the cab arrived at the house, she got out quickly, like a fugitive. She let herself in, grateful that no one would be home at this time of day. She wandered around the house like a person in a daze. It was strange seeing the house again. It looked familiar and unfamiliar all at once. Did she choose that gold flocked wall paper in the hall, those yellow chintz chairs in the sunroom? The place looked like something out of a designer magazine. There was stuff on every wall, every surface. She looked for a peaceful, uncluttered place to sit down but found none.

Retreating to the breakfast nook, she laid her head on the table. Lucy's dead face appeared before her. Alex had never seen anyone die. She cringed, remembering the awful guttural sounds Lucy had made. Earlier, Lucy had said she wasn't feeling well, but Alex hadn't thought anything of it, had kept talking, telling Lucy about Lockhart and Lockhart. She had even sent Lucy down to get a paper, thinking she could show the girl how to read the financial pages. The thought of Lucy running along the hall, her small heart straining, bursting at the seams, gave Alex an awful twisted feeling in the centre of her body. When Lucy rushed back into the room, she was out of breath. Then it happened. Her skin went as pale as ice, and there was a terrible choking sound. When Alex looked over, Lucy's arm had shot out and her hand was clutching out towards her.

Alex ran for the nurse, but by the time they raced back to the room, Lucy was staring at the ceiling, eyes inert. Lucy had died alone. Without anyone even holding her hand.

She felt bludgeoned by the memory of it. Dazed by the pain, she stared into the yard. There was a tree there and behind it, the old coach house perched on the edge of the ravine. When they had first bought the house, she'd been nervous about the ravine. All that wildness so close. She'd wanted to tear down the coach house too, but they'd never found time to do it.

Brrring. She jumped. The phone. Tom? Her father? Sue, her secretary? At the hospital, Sue had checked in with her every day. The ringing went on and on. Each ring felt like a reprimand. She should be calling people, letting them know where she was. She contemplated going upstairs, dressing in her best business suit and driving to the office. A good dose of work might snap her back into place. But everything about the office seemed irrelevant. Farcical. A woman had just died. Died. An entire life had been snuffed out in a matter of seconds. What could have meaning after that?

Alex stared at the paper someone had left open on the table. It was Saturday! Tom and the kids might appear at any moment. She couldn't let them see her like this. Her hands shook. Was this what it was like to go crazy? Truly frightened now, her eyes flew through the lush green yard to the coach house. Her body leaned towards it like a bird leans into the open sky.

•   •   •

After checking the phone several times and still not getting a dial tone, Jessie hobbled outside. The storm was over now, and the trees were full of mist and wetness from the rain. Water droplets hung from the branches like tiny silver tears. There was a long slab of grey rock by the water, and she made her way to it now to lie down. All her euphoria at being home had drained away. Pain shot up her leg from her foot.

She thought about Lucy. Had her family been informed yet? Probably.

Somewhere, people were grieving. Just as somewhere else, other people were laughing. And others, fighting.

"World is suddener than we fancy it, crazier and more of it than we think, incorrigibly plural..."

She wondered what Alex was feeling now. And where she was. She hardly knew the woman, yet felt a surge of kinship for her. The two of them had someone to mourn. She lay down on the rock, feeling the solid expanse of it against her back. Couldn't life ever be simple? Uncomplicated? Lately, one bad thing seemed to be happening after another. On the drive back home, Harley had told her there were more rumours about Price building something. What? Until they found out something more specific, there was nothing they could do. Nothing but worry.

Jessie made herself take some long, deep breaths and let her body sink down into the rock. There was something soothing about stone. It was consoling to know something that had been around for a long time. And had survived. She wondered about the variety of life this stone had seen. In the thousands of years of its existence, probably hundreds of animals had traversed it and in more recent decades, no doubt children had run across it, lovers had loved upon it, and many others, like her, had come to it in search of comfort. Feeling its comfort now, Jessie let the tears for Lucy wash through her. She wished that Alex had some nature to succour her. In times of hardship, there was nothing like climbing into the lap of nature.

She fell into a deep sleep and when she awoke, Harley was sitting quietly beside her. She told him about Lucy, and he nodded solemnly. Harley didn't get upset about death. To him, death was just another bend in the river.

He carried her back inside and took her into the bird room. In Elfy's hand was a bird no bigger than a thumb. It had a long, black bill not much thicker than a pine needle and around its throat was a triangular swath of luminescent red shaped like a cowboy's neckerchief. On its body were patches of featherless skin, grey and raw.

Jessie could see bits of glue and paper still stuck to the bird. "Is this the hummingbird that ran into the fly paper?" she asked

"Ruby," Elfy said nodding.

"She's a ruby-throated hummingbird," Harley said. "We've got about half the fly paper off now."

"How'd you get it off?" Jessie asked. She knew how strong the glue was on fly paper.

Elfy lifted a Q-tip. "Mineral oil and dish detergent and one heck of a lot of patience."

Jessie smiled. Patience wasn't something Elfy usually had in abundance. These birds must be teaching her a lot.

Elfy held the bird's bill with her thumb and ring finger and closed its eyes with the other two fingers, then began swabbing.

Jessie winced. "Imagine having all your feathers ripped

off like that and surviving!" The hummingbird's skin was raw and denuded, yet it seemed lively enough when Elfy slipped it back into its cage. "Will he fly again?"

"I called Maggie. She thinks he will," Elfy said. "But we have to keep him for a year. He can't migrate till he's molted, and right now, he ain't got nothing to molt." She began mixing some mash. "See, you didn't miss anything. It's feeding time again."

"I can see why you moved all the birds over here," Jessie said. "Seems to me you're either getting ready to feed, feeding or cleaning up from feeding."

"Listen to this," Elfy said and popped the plunger out of the syringe. At the sound the room exploded with bird squawking. Elfy grinned. "Alrighty, now, pipe down!" She moved near some finches that were no bigger than thimbles. "We should rename this place M.A.S.H. Here, help me get some of this grub into them, will you?"

Harley held their little heads while Jessie stuffed the mixture into their mouths. His hands looked huge beside the tiny bird heads. As Jessie fed them, she could feel her chest swell with warmth. What was it about small things that made them so endearing? Their vulnerability? It was amazing to think these tiny creatures had miniature stomachs, lungs and brains. And hearts that beat just like human hearts. She tried to imagine the size of the heart in the bird she was feeding. It was probably not much bigger than the head of a pea, yet she could see the way it made the bird's chest throb as it pumped. A tiny pulse in the vast percussion of nature.

Regardless of which bird she fed, the others stretched the Vs of their mouths wide. She smiled. Their eyes were still closed, yet they knew which direction the food was coming from. And shrieking that it wasn't coming fast enough.

"What happened to the mother of these ones?" Jessie asked.

"Cat," Elfy spat.

"Cats do what cats do," Harley said. "If that cat hadn't done what it had done, we wouldn't be here doing this."

Jessie put her open palm on Harely's back and felt the warmth of his skin through his shirt. To Harley, everything had its own place in the scheme of things. Life, death, hurt, joy, accidents. He made room for it all. For the most part, she liked that about him, but sometimes she found Harley's blind acceptance of things irritating. Wasn't it good not to accept things sometimes? If you accepted everything, the world would stay in the mess it was in.

Elfy frowned. "A hundred million."

"A hundred million?" Jessie asked.

"That's the number of birds that cats kill when they 'do what they do'," Elfy said.

Harley moved close to Elfy's face and meowed.

Elfy squirted a syringe of bird mash at him. "Gotcha. Right in the kisser!"

When all the birds had been fed, Jessie hopped back out to the phone. It was finally working. She called the hospital and gave the receptionist Alex's name. She smiled. Who would have thought she'd be *eager* to talk to Alex?

"No one by that name here, ma'am."

Jessie was incredulous. "Was she discharged?"

"The only information I have, ma'am, is that she is not a patient at this time."

"Oh." Jessie tried to keep the alarm out of her voice and hung up. Had Alex gone home? She called telephone information to see if she could get a listing for an A. Lockhart in Toronto, but the number was unlisted. Then she remembered that she had both women's addresses.

She wrote to Lucy's family first, expressing her grief and condolences. When the letter was finished, she picked out a hand-painted card and began a letter to Alex. At the end of it, she wondered if she should include the names of some therapists in Toronto. Would Alex be insulted if she did? Why was it that so many people thought the act of going to a therapist meant they weren't coping? Someone could be doing all kinds of neurotic things, but they would feel healthy as long as they were getting through it on their own.

"I'd rather handle it myself," Jessie had heard so many people say. What did people think? If they took their problems to a therapist, the therapist would get rid of the problems, like a garbage man took away the refuse? Goodness!

She sighed. No, she wouldn't mention therapy. Alex was perfectly capable of finding a therapist if she wanted one. She signed her name to the card, then added a postscript, "Remember, you're welcome to visit."

As soon as she wrote the words, she wanted to scratch them out. The last thing she needed was someone in crisis on her doorstep. Not on top of everything else. Besides, her grandson, Luke, was due to arrive any day now. And who knew what was going to happen with this situation with Price? Her stomach tightened just thinking about him.

She stared at the card unhappily. There was no way she could scratch out what she'd written. The only alternative was to write another note, and she was far too tired to do that.

Deciding that Alex wouldn't take up the offer anyway,

she went ahead and licked the envelope. Almost as soon as she had set it on the table, Elfy picked it up on her way into town. Jessie shook her head and hobbled to bed before anything else could happen.

·   ·   ·

Hoping no neighbours were watching, Alex made her way to the coach house. She'd only ever been in it once, just after they'd bought the house. Way back then, they'd promised themselves they were going to clean out the furniture, but they never had.

As she approached it now, it looked almost charming. The side facing the trees in the ravine was nearly all windows, the old-fashioned leaded ones with dozens of little panes. Growing over the roof and down the other side were long strands of ivy. The forest-green wooden door was rounded at the top. She pressed her thumb down on the wrought-iron latch, and the door swung open.

Inside, columns of sunlight sifted into the room. She stepped forward into the sweet aroma of old wood. Despite the mattress and other paraphernalia she saw piled in the corner, the room felt spacious and tranquil. She shut the door and leaned against it. This was probably the first time in her life that no one knew where she was. Poor Sue, her secretary, would be having a fit by now. Alex knew she should call, tell everyone not to worry, but she didn't feel capable of calling. She would cry if she called. She hadn't cried since she was six and wasn't going to start now.

Noticing a carpet rolled up in the corner, she dragged it out. The rug was sky blue, Persian, and had a filigree of apricot flowers around the edges. It was threadbare in the middle, but she waddled a heavy stone bird bath over the bare spot and it looked fine. In the centre of the bird bath was a ceramic angel playing a flute.

Then she saw the brass bed. She loved brass beds. This one was only a single, but she set it up against the back wall so that it faced the trees and pulled the mattress out. Behind the mattress was a pot-bellied wood stove like the one at her grandmother's cottage. Remembering the way her grandfather had put the curved metal handle in the cast-iron rings to lift them out, she did the same, then stuffed some old newspaper in the fire box as well as some small pieces of wood that were stacked nearby.

With trembling fingers, she tossed a match into the stove as if into a pile of explosives. The paper ignited the twigs and the smell of burning wood filled the room. She added some bigger bits of wood, then put the rings back in place and smiled. Smiled. How long it had been since she'd done that?

Rummaging around the various boxes, she found one containing rumpled sheets and an eiderdown. Pulling them out of their plastic wrapping, she made up the bed. Why was she doing this? When the bed was ready, she fell into it. Her eyes were wet. It was silly to react this way. People died. It was a fact of life. There was no sense getting upset about it.

She made herself breathe slowly as Jessie had done with her on the phone. As her chest moved up and down, she imagined she was floating. Floating in stillness. She liked this stillness. It soothed her, and when sleep came, she didn't fight it.

"Alex!"

She yanked open her eyes. The room was dark now.

Someone was standing in the doorway. A light flicked on, and the room was suddenly bright. Glaringly bright.

"What the hell's going on?" Tom's body looked giant in the small doorframe. "I went to the hospital. We've been looking everywhere! Calling—" He held up a fire extinguisher. "The smoke! I thought the place was on fire!" Shrugging, he put the extinguisher down and came over to her, pulling her to him fiercely. "I've been frantic." He stroked her hair. "I'm so glad you're all right." He pulled back and looked at the way she'd set up the room. "What's all...what's all this?"

Alex looked too, momentarily dazed, as if someone else had created this semblance of a home around her. She shook her head. She didn't know what to say.

He rose and tugged at her hands. "Come back to the house!"

Her body became a weight under his pulling. She tugged her hands free and covered her face. She couldn't face the house. The kids. Not right now. She cleared her throat. It felt dry again and sore.

"Tom, I need to think. I..." She could say no more. What she felt was far too big to wrap words around.

Tom searched her face as if looking for someone he knew. His voice was accusatory. "It's about that woman dying, isn't it?"

She shrugged. Yes. No. Understanding was beyond her now. "I need to be alone, I—Just for tonight. Please..." The last word died in her throat.

"But this is nuts!"

"Just give me a night. One night."

He sighed deeply. She could almost feel him crumpling. Slowly he moved toward the door. She wanted him to leave more than she ever wanted anything and felt ashamed that this was so.

Tom paused uncertainly as if he knew that once he retreated back across the threshold, nothing would ever be the same. "Your father had to send your secretary home in a cab. She was convinced you were dead. Said that was the only thing that would have stopped you from calling." He sighed, turned to go. "I'll let her know you're home."

Home. She repeated the word like an amnesiac. Home? What did it mean?

"Need me to bring you anything?"

She shook her head. Just go.

"Blankets? Some brandy? A hot water bottle?"

Her eyes stung. She imagined herself pushing him physically out the door and locking it. He gave her a long look then left. Relief swept over her. Then shame. Maybe her secretary was right. Maybe she had died. The Alex Lockhart everyone knew was nowhere to be found.

Chapter 6

J essie awoke to a boisterous chorus of birdsong.

"I'm moving into severe sleep deprivation," she said, pulling the pillow over her head. She hadn't slept past five a.m. since she'd been back. She opened her eyes. It was barely dawn, and already every beak was bursting with sound. How could such tiny bodies make so much noise?

Harley rolled towards her and nuzzled her back. She could tell he was awake. Or various parts of him were. Normally, they went to bed earlier, but last night they didn't turn in until after eleven because of a meeting in town. Then she'd been too riled up to sleep. She'd try to nap later, if that crazy kid wasn't racing his boat around the lake.

The meeting had been a farce. Right from the start, she'd had the feeling that the councillors had their minds made up in Price's favour. She shouldn't have listened to that clerk in the town office who told her Price's application for more docks would be turned down.

"Even the Ministry of Natural Resources opposes it," the clerk had told her, showing her the report. The report itself was clear and recommended that Price's shoreline application be rejected because of its negative affect on nesting sites. Why had she been so naïve to believe the town would listen to the MNR? Because everyone else who opposed it, herself included, didn't think Dick Price's application made sense. A lodge the size of Wildwood didn't need that many docks! Dick Price was obviously one of those "more is better" people, and she'd been certain the Town would see the stupidity of this kind of thinking and turn him down.

But Price had surprised them. First of all, he'd showed up with a big city lawyer. Then, when he didn't get his way, Price's lawyer came up with a loophole and changed their request from wanting *more* docks to extending the ones they had. Which was splitting hairs as far as Jessie could see. But the town gave its approval anyway. And now, this morning, Jessie felt as squashed as a flower underfoot. It was depressing.

Did birds get depressed? Did they suffer from anxiety and phobias and compulsions the way people did? Jessie didn't think so. As far as she could see, they were an incredibly intelligent species who brought nothing but beauty into the world.

"Sleep?" Harley asked.

She shook her head and yawned. She'd spent the night having one imaginary argument after another with Price, his lawyer and the Town.

Harley pulled her gently on top of him and she lay her head on his chest, grateful for the solace of his body. The calm spread of him was soothing. Slowly he massaged her back, then other places until her whole body thrummed.

"You've got me chirping now," she said when they finally got up. She made her way to the bird room. She knew she should do her foot exercises first, but there never seemed to be time. She certainly couldn't do them with the birds squawking like this. They sounded like a thousand fingernails scraping on a blackboard.

Despite her tiredness, as she began to feed the birds, an

easy contentment moved through her. She loved feeding them, loved the way their mouths stretched wide as funnels, loved the intensity and purity of their need to survive.

When they were finished, she fell back in her chair, exhausted and hungry. "I'm starving." Harley held out a spoonful of mealy worms. She laughed and stood up. "I'm not that far gone. Yet."

"Speaking of far gone," Elfy said, appearing in the doorway. Yesterday, they'd said they were going to clean cages, and she was here to help. She rubbed her elbow.

"What's the matter with your arm?" Jessie asked

"Touch of arthritis," Elfy said. "It ain't fair. I spend all these years getting my head together, and my body starts falling apart."

Jessie laughed. "Come on, let's have some tea." She hobbled into the kitchen.

Elfy followed. "Cheep, cheep."

As Jessie put on the kettle, the phone rang.

"Leave it, Elf—"

But Elfy had already picked it up. Jessie frowned and made some toast.

She listened as Elfy tried to sort out what sounded like someone with an abandoned bird. Elfy said just what she would have said, that even though it might look as if the parents had left the bird, that wasn't necessarily so. Elfy advised them not to touch it, but to watch the bird and see if the parents returned, which they did ninety percent of the time. Like Elfy, Jessie knew that if the people actually touched the bird, it was probably going to lead to an admission. And they didn't need any more admissions. Not only was the refuge full to bursting, but they were exhausted. Besides, it was far better for the bird to stay in its own habitat.

"You did pick it up?"

Jessie heard Elfy sigh.

"Just make sure you don't feed it then," Elfy said. "Don't—you what? Oh. What did you feed it?"

Elfy sounded irritated now, and Jessie could feel her own tension rising. What they fed it would decide whether or not the bird lived. All too often, when people found a bird, they tried to act like surrogate parents and fed the bird worms. What people didn't understand was how dangerous the bacteria in those worms were, so dangerous to the bird's survival that the saliva in parent birds contained a special anti-bacterial property to neutralize it. So, if a mother fed a baby bird a worm, that was all right, but if a person fed a baby bird a worm, the bird was likely to die.

"You fed it WHAT?" Elfy put her hand over the phone. "The bonehead fed the bird milk!"

Jessie sighed. The bird didn't have much of a chance of surviving now. It was sad. If only people would call them *before* they did things with birds.

"No! Tell me you didn't." Elfy was almost shouting now. "Breast milk? You fed it BREAST MILK?"

It was the ultimate hubris. Feeding another species what yours would require.

"When was the last time you saw frigging breasts on a bird!" Elfy pulled the phone away from her ear, then brought it back. "She hung up!"

Jessie sighed. "Elfy, take it easy!"

"Oh, for crying out loud! Breast milk. How stupid can you get?"

"Yes, it was stupid, but she didn't know. She was only trying to help."

"She *helped*, all right. Helped the bird *die*." She collapsed into a chair, her face in her hands.

Jessie sat down heavily beside her. Up until a few weeks ago, she might have fed an abandoned bird milk too. It was a common mistake to make. What was discouraging about such a mistake was that it showed just how out of tune the general population was with nature and wild things.

Jessie put her hand on Elfy's head. The old woman's hair felt dry and wiry.

"Come. Drink your tea," Jessie said.

Elfy sat up slowly and accepted the cup Jessie poured for her. Listlessly, she began looking at some of the books spread out on the table. "These for your course?" She read the titles. "*Identification of North American Birds, Bird Behaviour, The Complete Birder...*they don't sound very psychological."

Jessie shrugged. She hadn't looked at her school books in weeks.

"This looks interesting," Elfy said, pointing to a book on geese.

"It is! Know why geese fly in formation?"

Never one to hold on to a mood for long, Elfy said, "'Cause V's the only letter of the alphabet they know?"

Jessie smiled. "The V creates an uplift for the bird behind. That way they get better mileage."

"Imagine!"

"And when the front one gets tired, it goes to the back and another comes forward."

"Sharing the driving." Elfy said. She yawned as Harley sat down at the table. "I'm tuckered right out."

"Makes two of us," Harley said.

Over the last while, they'd taken in far more birds than they'd ever expected: baby birds, injured birds, birds tossed out of the nest. They were taking them in faster than they were able to fix them and release them. Jessie pulled a chair up and rested her leg on top.

Elfy frowned and looked at Jessie. "You look knackered too!"

"I feel knackered."

"Still not sleeping, eh?"

"Nope."

"Maybe we should give ourselves a break," Elfy said, looking at Harley. "Not take any new birds for a while..."

"No!" Jessie said. She loved working with birds. More than she wanted to admit. *"You only have to let the soft animal of your body love what it loves..."*

"What in heaven's name—"

"It's from a poem."

"How about we put a closed sign up for a few days," Elfy said.

Jessie didn't want to, but knew they needed to catch up with themselves.

Harley spread open the newspaper. "We'll cut the phone lines."

Elfy grinned. "Put a moat around the place."

"Throw in some 'gators."

Elfy chuckled.

Jessie took a long sip of tea and watched as Harley poured his into a beer mug. When he had tea, he liked plenty of it. Then he dipped his spoon into the blond cream of the honey jar, scooped a mound out and stirred it in as he turned over the paper.

"Shit!"

Jessie's eyes jumped to the headline Harley was pointing at and read it aloud. "New Golf Course Planned For Wildwood."

Elfy shot forward in her seat.

Jessie carried on reading. "A new golf course is planned at Wildwood Lodge. Mr. Price, the owner, an avid golfer, says he plans to build a state of the art, eighteen-hole course and club house which will attract golfers from all over the continent."

"That explains the architect's fees," Harley said. "And the extra docks!"

"Bastard!" Elfy said.

"Just what we need—another golf course," Jessie said. There were twenty-one in the area already, and she'd heard there were proposals for a dozen more. She looked over at the pines on the Wildwood estate and cringed. "I've nothing against golf, but do we have to have a golf course for every man, woman and child? Do you know how many trees have to be destroyed for one eighteen-hole golf course?"

"Don't want to, neither." Elfy said.

Jessie tried to calculate the amount of acreage an eighteen-hole golf course would require and whether Price was going to need the land their house was on.

Elfy was obviously thinking the same way. "Why do I feel the end of a boot coming our way?"

"And not just us," Jessie said. "For every bird, squirrel, racoon, deer, snake…"

"Someone should blow his house up, see how he likes that!" Elfy banged her fist on the table. "Time for the Grannies!"

Jessie knew what calling The Grannies meant: a full-scale protest involving strategy meetings, press releases, interviews and public debates. How were they going to find time for that?

Elfy stood up. "I'm going to start rounding people up."

Jessie put her head down on the table and closed her eyes. It was all too much. She heard Elfy's chair scraping against the wooden floor. After the screen door banged, Harley put his hand on hers. She stared longingly into the bird room. All she wanted was to sprout wings and fly far, far away.

•   •   •

In the dream, Alex felt her face coming off. Great sheets of it were peeling away. It was strange because Alex could watch it happening, like she was watching a snake shed its skin, yet she could feel it at the same time. When the excoriation was done, she walked over to the mirror but awoke before seeing who she'd become.

Normally, Alex didn't remember dreams. She wished she hadn't remembered this one. Wanting to put it from her mind, she made coffee and brought a cup back to bed. In the quiet of the dawn, she heard her watch alarm go off somewhere in the room. *Get up, get to work,* the watch bleeped. Just a week ago, she would have been in the shower by now. She lay there listening to the bleeping, waiting for it to stop.

Why she even bothered with a watch had always puzzled her. Inevitably, she knew the time. It was as if she had a built in timepiece, tick, tick, ticking away inside her, like the alligator in Peter Pan who swallowed the clock.

When she couldn't stand the bleeping anymore, she tracked down the watch, opened the round-topped door and hurled the watch into the ravine. Guilt grabbed her. Her father had given her that watch as a reward for landing the Fitzgerald account. Her father. She felt her shoulders tense.

As a child, her father used to make her stand in front of the mirror and practise her smile. Putting on a smile was important to her father. He called it "face patrol". More like face *control,* she thought, sipping her coffee. But when someone died in front of you, the whole idea of control became a hoax. There was no such thing as control. Yet her whole life had been built on the premise that there was.

She had tried to explain this to Tom when he came in last night. He was trying his best to understand why she was still out here, but was obviously having difficulty. "I can understand you not going to work," he'd told her. "You're still getting better, but, why can't you stay in the house with the rest of us?"

Because I need to be alone, she wanted to scream at him as her body had been screaming at her.

But she didn't scream. She simply became silent. And Tom had become silent too, then walked away, shaking his head.

Now, in the early morning, she lay in bed listening to the birds. What a variety of sounds they made: whistles, cackles, caws, chirps, warbles, trills, zips and beeps. She wished she had binoculars so she could figure out which bird was making what sound. There were binoculars up at the house and other things she needed, but she'd been putting off going there. Tom or the kids had been bringing her what she needed, but she couldn't put off having a shower one more day. Besides, today she was feeling strong. When she was sure the house would be empty, she crossed the yard to the back door.

Turning the brass doorknob, she felt as if she were sneaking into someone else's home. Inside, she tiptoed through the breakfast nook, glancing at the telephone. The answering machine flashed its red light. It flashed according to how many calls there were. Obviously, no one had cleared them in days. She stopped counting at fifteen. Once upon a time, that would have made her feel important. Now it made her feel tense.

She thought for a moment about calling Jessie again. As good as it would be to hear Jessie's calming voice, now that she was coping, she wanted to keep her distance from anything psychological. Besides, she knew if she called, all her feelings about Lucy would rush back and she didn't want that.

Still feeling furtive, she climbed the thickly carpeted steps. Quickly, she packed an old brown pullover and a few pairs of slacks and underwear. She left all the stylish things behind. Then she took a shower. Usually she wore a shower cap to protect her hair—Anton, her hairdresser, didn't like her to touch it. But today, she let the hot, steamy water pour over her, then washed her hair and towelled it dry. She wanted to see what it would look like without Anton's potions and sprays. He liked to blow-dry it slick and straight, but now, left to itself, it curled rambunctiously as it had when she'd been little.

"This is me," she whispered to the mirror. She had a startled, wild look, like an animal suddenly released from a cage. What would the people at the office think of this, she wondered. Her father, she knew, would hate it.

In the kitchen, she packed potatoes, onions, carrots, lettuce and rice into a bag and added a few old pots. It was time to start feeding herself instead of relying on the soup and sandwiches Tom brought. When everything was ready, she took the binoculars from the shelf above the breakfast nook.

The doorbell rang. Her body went rigid. The mailman? Delivery boy? She was not going to answer it. *Go away. Alice doesn't live here anymore.* The bell rang again, in a commanding sort of way, as if the person outside knew she was there on the inside. Her shoulders tightened. Edging into the dining room, she peeked out the window. It was Angus! Her father! He was standing within feet of her, his hands on his hips.

He rang the bell again. Her insides leapt in fear, but her feet stayed frozen in place. What was she going to do? It felt dangerous being so close to him. Forcing herself to move, she tip-toed back into the kitchen, gathered her things and slipped out the back.

"Where do you think you're going?"

She dropped the bag and heard the pots clatter. Slowly she turned. She tried to get herself to speak, but the consternation on his face stopped her. She saw what he saw. Some wild-haired woman without make-up, dressed in old jeans, a sweatshirt and beat-up tennis shoes. His eyes said, *Who is this?* She watched his face, saw him assess her, pick a plan of action. She'd seen him do this with clients a hundred times.

His eyes grabbed hers firmly as if she were an unruly child. "I know the situation at the hospital upset you, but..."

She cringed. Lucy's dying was a "situation"?

"You've got to pick up the ball and keep going. Get back in the game."

She felt her muscles weaken and worried she might sink to the ground. She knew if she did, her father would come over and pull her up, pep-talk her like a boxer who'd taken too many punches.

"You can do it, Al!"

The mantra of the motivated. *You can do it.* He had said these words to her a thousand times. To conquer math tests, soccer games, hurt feelings...

His eyes narrowed. "Come on, Al!"

Why didn't you come and visit me? The words were hot in her throat, but she could not say them. She thought about Lucy and dropped her eyes.

"Maybe I should send over Dr. Medler."

Her eyes leapt to his in fear. Not Dr. Medler. He belonged to her mother.

No. She didn't know if she actually said the word, but she felt it in her chest, hard as a stone. She wanted to pull it out and fling it at him. She looked at her father warily. For the first time in her life, she realized he might be dangerous to her.

Switching tacks, he waved his hands, then arranged his fingers into guns, aimed them towards her and fired. "Get better, then."

Alex took a sharp breath. They stood, not speaking. Then he shifted slightly on his feet, and she thought he might move toward her. She imagined him taking her into his arms and holding her. Just for once, she wanted *not* to be strong, *not* to be motivated. Just for once, she wanted to be the scared person she was. Give me this. A guillotine of rationality came over his eyes, severing the impulse. His face became hard and immutable. He walked away.

It took Alex a long time to drag herself back to the coach house. When she was safely inside, she locked the door behind her.

Chapter 7

Despite her aching foot, Jessie tromped through the woods. Her foot wasn't really well enough for her to do this, but she had to move, had to get rid of her anger somehow. Around her were hundreds of trees, maples, oaks, pines and beeches, some with trunks so wide she could wrap her arms around them, others so slender, they were no bigger than her wrist. Wide or thin, tall or short, they were all going to be destroyed. In the thicket of boughs, she could hear robins, finches and jays. When their habitat was wiped out, the birds would go too.

A deer bolted from behind a log and she stood still, watching its white rump bounce through the air. It saddened her the way this animal ran in terror at the sight of her. To the deer, she was dangerous. As were all humans. She felt ashamed that this was so.

It infuriated her to live in a society where one man was permitted to obliterate a forest like this. And for what? To whack around a golf ball? It was obscene. Unless Jessie and The Grannies spent every last bit of their energy fighting Price, he was going to get away with it. He was probably going to get away with it anyway, she thought bitterly. Like most of the people who pushed for "progress", Price was powerful enough to squelch those who raised a hand of protest. But raise a hand of protest she would. What choice did she have?

She wouldn't be able to live with herself otherwise.

She picked up a rusty pop tin, put it in her knapsack and walked on.

Garbage, there was always garbage. Then, seeing a plastic juice bottle, she kicked it. Purple liquid shot out the end as it arced in the air, then landed behind a rock. She wanted to leave it but couldn't. Sighing heavily, she retrieved it and stuffed it on top of the other things in her backpack. Why did she have to clean up after everyone else? And fight Price! It wasn't fair! Who was running this Universe anyway?

Although she had never been able to buy the idea of an up-in-the-sky-old-man kind of God, she did believe there was an Intelligence that had its hand in things. Something had to have created this incredible beauty and diversity all around her. But if there was an Intelligence, why couldn't it make her life easier? She was one of the good guys, for goodness sakes. Surely, her life shouldn't be this hard. How were they going to run a bird refuge *and* a campaign?

Elfy thought they should close down the refuge for a few months and devote all their energy to fighting the Wildwood development, but Jessie loathed the idea of giving up the birds. Harley, on the other hand, was talking about selling everything and finding some wilderness, while there was still some left to find. The question was, what was the right thing to do here? She wanted a sign. A clear sign.

When her foot was too sore to go on, she hobbled back to the house. Inside, she could hear bird cages opening and closing. She was emptying her knapsack when Elfy came out of the bird room.

"The meeting's all set up."

"The meeting?"

Irritation pulled at Elfy's mouth. "With The Grannies. It's not till the tenth, 'cause Aggie's away. She'd roast me naked if we had it without her."

"Okay," Jessie said.

"Meanwhile, like I said, let's keep the refuge closed." She looked hard at Jessie and saw her reluctance. "Jessie, don't be a bone-head. You could fix a thousand birds, and it won't do a damn bit of good if their habitats get wiped out. And that's what's going to happen if we don't stop Price. There won't be a branch for a bird left."

She was right, of course. Jessie knew that. She'd read the ecological reports. They all said the same thing: loss of habitat was the biggest threat to life on the planet—over global warming, over car emissions, over everything.

"Look," Elfy said. "It's not forever. We'll get it up and running after we whip Price's backside."

There was the sound of car tires on the gravel driveway. An approaching car usually meant someone was arriving with a wounded bird, but Harley had put a "Temporarily closed" sign down by the road, so Jessie didn't think it was that. Who was it then? Dick Price delivering an eviction notice?

She heard the *whoomph* of a car door slamming.

"Expecting anyone?" Harley asked, coming in from his leatherwork.

Elfy swatted Harley's arm. "Quick. Lock the door."

They stood perfectly still, waiting. There was a soft knock at the door, the kind a child might make. The three of them looked at each other, and Harley stepped forward.

"Harley!" Elfy reached out to stop him, but it was too late. He opened the door. There, in the opening stood a young boy holding a cardboard box close to his chest. Beside him was a man who looked like the boy's father.

"We're shut," Elfy called out. "Didn't ya see the sign?"

The boy's lower lip trembled.

Hearing faint peeping sounds, Jessie eyed the box. She willed herself not to look inside. The man and boy would just have to take care of what was inside the box themselves. Isn't that what people had done before the bird refuge had been founded?

"I hate to tell you this folks, but we're closed for a while," Harley said.

The man, tall with sandy hair, nodded gravely. A baby-like chirp came through the air holes in the box. The bird sounded as if it were starving. Had they fed it? Jessie pressed her lips together. She would not ask.

"Oh, for crying out loud," Elfy said, stepping forward. "At least we can tell these people what to feed the darned thing."

Jessie watched the boy's face soften and the man smile as Elfy peeked inside.

"It's a loon! A baby loon!" Her voice softened into an adoring croon.

One down, Jessie thought, willing herself not to look.

"There were two chicks," the man said. "But the parents abandoned this one almost right after it was born. We thought they'd come back for it."

"We waited five whole hours," the boy said.

"Sure sounds hungry," Elfy said. "We'll give you some food, something you can feed it at home."

Jessie watched Harley peer into the box, saw his lips pull to one side in the way they did when he wasn't hopeful. Guessing that the creature inside was on its last legs and that they wouldn't be able to do much, Jessie decided to allow herself a quick peek.

There, sitting on some towelling, was a small ball of black fluff with a tiny beak sticking out one end and two little eyes above. The baby loon peered at her hopefully and made a plaintive cry. Jessie put her hand to her heart before it cracked open like a shell, then closed the box firmly.

"I'm sorry, we can't help you."

That's what she intended to say. She looked at the man.

"Leave it with us." She knew a sign when one hit her in the face.

• • •

Alex took a handful of bird seed and let it sift into the feeder through her closed hand as though through an hour glass. She'd rigged up several bird feeders made out of jar lids and pieces of bark and had suspended them with string from various branches around the coach house. The birds were getting used to her now and didn't fly so far away when she filled them. They seemed unperturbed when she sat and watched them with her binoculars.

The feeders swung in the wind, but the birds landed on them anyway. She marvelled at their ability to move with the unpredictability of the wind. Birds were certainly creatures of the moment. She wished she could be the same, push the past and future aside, like curtains, and live in the light of the present. It would be so freeing. So often her mind was occupied with what *had* happened or what *might* happen. This morning, for example, she couldn't get Dr. Medler out of her mind.

Her father wouldn't just send him over, would he? She remembered the day Dr. Medler had come to assess her mother, the way he entwined his small, knobby fingers near his face like a squirrel. The first time he'd come, Alex had been eight. She'd hidden behind the couch so she could listen. The questions he had asked had confused her. Why did he need to know how often her mother washed her hands? Or heard voices? Listening from her hiding place, it had been all she could do not to run out and lead her mother back to her bedroom. She had hated that her mother just sat staring down at her feet as if they were nailed to the ground.

Ever since, Alex had been nervous around psychiatrists. Even in her professional relationship with them as clients, she was ill at ease, disliking the way they nodded after everything she said, as if sorting her words into different psychological categories. Their questions always sounded drilling, like they were dentists of the mind. She wanted nothing to do with them.

But what if Dr. Medler simply appeared unannounced at her door? The thought frightened her. *Come on,* the logical side of her brain said, *he's not going to just show up. You're being paranoid.* As adamant as the voice was, she had less faith in the cerebral part of her brain than before and, deciding she wanted to prepare for all possibilities, she considered her options. If he did come, the most obvious possibility, and by far the most desirable, was simply not to see him. But, God, what would the consequences be of that? Her mental health was already in question: she'd run away from the hospital, moved out here, and wasn't showing up for work. Would they try and commit her? Is that what Dr. Medler would try to do?

Her mind ransacked what she'd learned in law school. It wasn't so easy to commit someone, if she remembered correctly. But she'd seen the way Dr. Medler had wheedled things out of her mother. What if he found out she had more interest in looking at the birds than stock market figures? Or that she'd had thoughts of living out here permanently? Was that enough to put her in one of those white places, where nurses pushed pill trolleys down sanitized hallways? Would she have to undergo the vicious jolts of shock treatments like her mother? Her mother had withstood dozens, all justified as necessary kick-starts to get her back into the world.

A new thought entered her awareness. What if her mother hadn't wanted to be a part of the world? What if her mother's illness wasn't really an illness at all, but an inadvertent way of allowing her to stay in her own small world in her own small way? Was that so crazy? Perhaps not, but her mother had paid dearly for it.

Then another thought came, but this one scared her. Would they think she was crazy because her mother was? Weren't there certain types of mental illness that ran in families? Thoroughly intimidated now, she resolved, if the doctor did come, to do her best to sound rational. And cooperative. If she was cooperative, she was sure she would be permitted this blip of dysfunction. If she swallowed her medication and was good, she might be allowed to bypass the mental hospital route and go back to work. People at the office would whisper about her little "episode", but the gossip wouldn't last. As long as she pressed her foot down on the accelerator of success and sped back into the race, people would give her another chance. Her father would make them.

But did she want another chance? She thought about Evan. Last weekend, he'd come out here and the two of them had played cards, watched birds and talked. She'd felt close to him in a way she never had before. She had laughed at his silly jokes, and she could feel him relax with her in a way he hadn't before. In the past, she'd always seen her time with her children as "kid duty", something she was required to do, all the while yearning to be back at the office where the important work was. How ridiculous, she thought now.

When Evan had left, he'd kissed her. She touched her cheek as if to feel the warmth of it again. She wished now there weren't so few years left in his childhood. She'd already missed so many. But it wasn't too late. Not like it was with Christina. She'd already lost Christina's childhood. Traded it for stock options.

Of her two children, Alex knew Christina was having the more difficult time accepting her coach house retreat. She didn't expect Christina to understand. How could she? Alex didn't understand it herself. Yet Evan seemed to accept her being out here. Perhaps Christina would too.

As Alex watched the birds in her binoculars, she saw a mother trying to teach one of its young to fly. The mother kept demonstrating how to do it by flying off and returning, flying off and returning. The baby bird stood uncertainly on the limb, moving from one foot to the other. Poor thing, she thought. It was being asked to step off the branch into the abyss of air, trusting that some instinct would take over and show it what to do. She understood its fear completely.

• • •

As soon as the boy and his father had left, Harley began moving the couches around. Jessie stood holding the box with the loon protectively.

"What are you doing?"

"Making a nest." He spread plastic garbage bags over the joined couches. "Don't worry, birds don't foul their nest. The couch won't get dirty."

When towels had been spread over the plastic to make it soft, Jessie lifted the tiny bird from the box. It was like lifting a ball of air. The loon had a stark white underbelly and two black webbed feet that looked about two sizes too big. They were as black as rubber boots. She eased the loon gently down on the towels and withdrew her hand. He stood up quickly and tried to walk toward her.

Elfy looked worried, but smiled. "He walks like a clown with flipper feet."

"Think 'paddles'," Harley said.

Not designed to walk on land, the loon's feet were positioned far back on its body. Each foot had three "fingers" and two wide, pie-shaped wedges of webbing in between. Despite how difficult it was for him to walk, the loon trudged up Jessie's arm anyway. His feet made little splatting sounds on her skin as he went. "Where you going?" she whispered to him. He was adorable.

"Careful," Elfy said.

"What?"

"You're sounding gooey."

"Gooey?"

"Gooey! Gagga! Lovey-dovey!"

The loon made little peeping sounds. "I think he's hungry," Jessie said. "What do loons eat? Minnows?"

"By the truckload," Harley said. "Be right back."

"While he's getting some fish, I'll call Maggie," Elfy said. "See what she has to say." She headed off.

Jessie stroked the bird's head with her index finger. "Minnows by the truckload? A little thing like you?" The loon crawled up to the crook of her arm now and huddled into her chest. She looked down at it, hardly able to believe it was real. The faint pulse of its heart beat against her skin. The loon pecked at her hand anxiously.

"The minnow man is on his way." She petted the baby's head in an attempt to soothe it. Not wanting to intrude on its world, she was nervous about touching it. After all, it was a different species, and she wanted to respect that. Besides, it wasn't a good idea for wild things to become too familiar with people, she thought, remembering what had happened with their neighbour a few years ago.

Mrs. Quinn, an elderly woman, had taken in a baby wolf, treating it like a pet. When the old woman had to go into a home, she'd let the wolf free. Used to getting food from people, the wolf had approached some cottagers. Thinking the wolf's friendliness meant it was rabid, they had shot and killed it.

The loon cried out and pushed his head against Jessie's arm, reminding her that regardless of the fact that she and it were different species, he was, after all, still a baby and needed contact. She thought about Luke, her grandson, who was arriving in a day or two.

"Luke will love you," she said, as she stroked the loon's head with her index finger. The chick leaned into the caress, then fixed its eyes on her.

"What are you staring at?" She yawned. Goodness, she was tired.

She'd heard that baby birds made parents out of the first moving figures they saw. Was the loon committing her face to memory as "Mamma Loon"? She smiled. Mamma Loon. Really.

"You must think I've got a funny looking beak, huh?"

The bird pecked her hand again.

She spread her fingers. "I've got funny looking feet too. Look—no webs. Weird, eh?"

The loon stared at her intently. Hadn't she read somewhere that loons were the oldest birds on earth?

Elfy watched her from the doorway. She sighed. "Told you not to get attached. This guy doesn't have a snowball's chance in hell."

"Who says?" Jessie yawned again.

"Maggie had me call this loon expert in the States."

"What did he say?" Jessie pulled her eyes from the loon to Elfy.

"He said to euthanize it."

"Put it to sleep?" Anger exploded in her chest. "Why?"

"Said a loon can't live away from its parents. Said we might as well put it out of its misery."

"Did this *expert* tell you what we should do if we don't euthanize it?"

"He suggested we contact the zoo. See if they'll take it."

"What did Maggie say?"

Elfy grimaced. "I was getting to that. She said for the loon to have a chance, we'd have to become its parents— eat with it, sleep with it, basically stay with it twenty-four hours a day. Even then the chances are slimmer than slim."

"Twenty-four hours a day! No way!"

"You're crazy-tired as it is!" Elfy said.

"Be nuts to even consider it."

Jessie looked down at the loon. "Good thing for you I'm not afraid of being nuts."

"Jessie, no!"

Jessie shook her head. "I can't send this little guy away. I can't."

Elfy crossed her arms. "You're asking for it. Just downright asking for it." She pressed her lips together. "Let me call the zoo. Just to see."

"Elfy, I have to do what I have to do."

Harley strode in with a bucket. Reaching his wide hand into the water, he pulled out one of the long silver minnows. "Sushi!" he said, swinging it by the tail. He offered it to the loon who swallowed it in one voracious gulp.

"Ohhhh, look! See the way he ate that?" Elfy grinned.

Jessie put her hand to her temple. It felt as if someone was having a tantrum with their fists on her skull.

Harley watched her. "Another headache? Why don't you go and lie down?"

"At least his appetite's good," Elfy said, giving the loon another minnow.

"Be a bucket a day in no time," Harley said.

"That's a lot of minnows for the parents to catch," Jessie said. "Didn't the man say there were two chicks? How come the parents abandoned one?"

Harley shrugged. "Think how much time a loon has to be under water to feed two babies. On a busy lake, that would jeopardize both chicks. So, the parents pick one and leave the other. That way, at least one survives."

Jessie's face darkened. "You mean this chick was abandoned because there are too many boats on the lake?"

The banging in her head became more violent.

"Basically," Harley said.

Elfy scowled. "Mother of Jesus, father of Christ! Doesn't that make you want to sock that kid in the kisser?" She reached for another minnow. "I suppose we're lucky the parents didn't abandon both babies." The loon swallowed the minnow as easily as if it were a lozenge of oil. "This guy sure likes his raw fish. Maybe we should call him Sushi."

Harley and Elfy both turned to Jessie, but Jessie was looking out over the lake, her face bunched into a fist.

• • •

The warm, early morning sun pressed itself against her body like a hug. Alex sat, her back leaning against the shed wall. Her thighs felt like thick ropes, well-worked from pulling her up the sides of the ravine. It felt good getting acquainted with her body again, as if she was reconnecting with an important relative she had lost touch with.

The birds on her feeders suddenly scattered. Hearing hard shoes on the walk, she looked up. Tom, dressed in the full regalia of the business world, grey suit, striped tie, dark socks and polished black shoes, was striding towards her. He handed her some mail, then went into the coach house. She followed, laid the envelopes on the table and watched as Tom sat down tiredly. Even though his day had yet to begin, his face was stiff with tension.

For a moment, she flashed on her first sighting of him at Camp Ahmanee, bronzed and grinning as he paddled toward her that summer so many years ago. She had fallen in love with him the moment she'd seen him. Both camp counsellors, they used to sneak away at night and meet up on the cliff. She smiled, remembering how sleep-deprived they had become after a few weeks of knowing each other.

Alex looked at Tom now, and a great yearning moved through her. She was grateful to him for giving her this time in the coach house and not pressuring her. Not many husbands would have cut their wives so much slack. Besides, it was a beautiful morning, and she felt better than she had in days. On impulse, she leaned towards him and kissed his cheek. The soft bareness of his skin surprised her. She reached up and loosened his tie. The cloth of it felt silky in her fingers. She moved her mouth to his and thought how lovely it would be to feel his bare chest against her breasts again. It had been a long time.

She felt him tense.

"Al—"

"I could call in," she whispered. When they were first married, they used to call in sick to each others' bosses, then stay in bed and make love all day.

Tom pulled away. The stark blueness of his crisp cuff flashed as he raised his arm to straighten his tie.

Quickly she covered her naked hope and sat back in her chair. She couldn't look at him. Something was happening she didn't understand.

"Dr. Medler is coming."

She jerked her head up. "Dr. Medler? When?"

"Any minute." Tom put his face in his hands, digging the ends of his fingers into his eye sockets. "This is your father's doing, not mine." He sighed and blew air out his mouth. "I wasn't supposed to tell you."

He pushed his hands against the table as if to lift the great weight of what was on his shoulders. "I couldn't do that." He was standing now. "But I do think you should see him. You've been out here almost three weeks now. It's not—" He stopped, changed his words. "He might be able to help, that's all. It can't hurt."

Alex felt her body go cold. The word "hurt" repeated like an echo. She swallowed. Then swallowed again. Had it been three weeks? She was losing track of time. For all she knew, she might be losing track of other things too. What if she was going crazy after all? Tears gathered in her eyes. She willed them back and looked down.

On his way out, Tom reached over and squeezed her arm, but her arm felt dead. He shut the door quietly, as if on a sick person.

Alex stared dully around the room, then began to pace. She needed to pull herself together! What was she going to say? At the very least, she must stop pacing. She must look crazy traipsing up and down the room like this. Calm down! But she couldn't calm down. Danger was too near.

Her eyes raced around the room, landing on the mail Tom had left. The name "Dearborn" caught her eye. She tore open the envelope. The card was a hand-painted scene of water and pine trees. Inside, she grabbed on to the words like a life ring. The words were: "welcome to visit." She scanned the rest of the letter, then lowered her arm, still gripping the card. Knowing she had only moments, she stood up, put some clothes into a bag, scribbled a note to Tom.

You can't keep running away like this! *It's crazy. Crazy!*

Keeping her head down as if she might have to plow through an opponent, she rushed outside and along the path. She passed someone wearing shiny black shoes. The shiny black shoes stopped, and she heard her name. She kept going. There was a lot of freedom in crazy.

Chapter 8

Jessie felt sore all over. She had just finished doing the night shift with Sushi, and, as always, she'd been so nervous about rolling over and crushing him, she'd hardly slept. Finally, near dawn, just as exhaustion was dragging her into a light doze, Sushi squawked for his first feed and woke her. She couldn't remember what she was dreaming, but the dark, foreboding feeling of it clung to her.

"Give me a minute, Sush. As soon as I can get this wet sand bag of a body moving, I'll get you breakfast."

Harley had already left to do the minnow run, but hopefully there were a few fish to get Sushi started. Keeping Sushi in minnows was turning out to be a job in itself. He was eating a few dozen every day and, even though Orf, the bait man, was giving them a discount, the cost of them was daunting. And going to get them every day was just one more job that had to be done.

The phone rang.

"No!"

She wasn't ready for the phone to ring this early. Between wounded birds, house guests, Sushi, clients, this place was a circus. She felt pushed to her limit. "Stop," she shouted at the phone. Why wasn't the answering machine answering? It was all she could do not to throw the phone across the room. If she didn't get a good night's sleep soon, she was going to go crazy.

This is how it happens, she thought. The rubber band of sanity gets stretched and stretched until one day, it snaps. Don't. Don't think this way. She sighed and reached for the phone.

"Seen this morning's paper?" Aggie asked tersely.

"I haven't seen my toothbrush."

"Call me when you do."

"Welcome home—" Aggie hung up before Jessie could finish the sentence. What had put Aggie's nose out of joint?

"Want me to feed him, Gran?" Luke, tall but thin for his twelve years, stood in the doorway. He hadn't changed out of his bathing suit since he'd arrived. She patted the couch beside her and he rushed over, his eyes fixed on the loon. Jessie kissed his tanned forehead and smiled. "Sure." Who was she to stand in the way of young love? "Why don't you take him to the pool? Feed him there." She watched Luke pick up the loon with tender care and carry him outside.

When Sushi had first arrived, they had let him swim in the bathtub, but when he had kept banging into the sides, they'd splurged and bought a large upright pool, five feet deep, that they could swim in as well. Sushi, of course, loved the pool, and even though he still slept inside, the rest of the time he insisted on being out in it.

The phone rang again. This time it was a fisherman reporting a heron with a lure caught in its mouth. Jessie wrote down where the man had seen the bird and told him they'd get out there as soon as Harley was back. Almost as soon as she put down the phone, it rang again. It was

John, one of her clients, asking if he could have an extra session this week.

"I've been feeling agitated," he said.

SO HAVE I, she wanted to shout. Unfortunately, she had to tell him there was nothing extra available this week. Then, because she felt guilty for being so busy, she spent a few more minutes with him to make sure he was all right. Her foot ached. She needed to do her exercises, but when?

Finished with the call, she lay back. She must have dozed off again, because when she woke up a few minutes later she could hear someone in the kitchen.

"We're out of bird mash," Elfy called.

"Check in the broom closet," Jessie called. "I think there's some in there."

Jessie heard Elfy grumble and pulled herself up. Through the kitchen window she could see Luke running to the pool in his bare feet, a sloshing minnow bucket at the end of one arm. Wanting to watch him, she made herself some tea and took it outside and sat on the side of the pool, her feet dangling in the water. Luke dropped a minnow into the water. Sushi torpedoed after it, then gulped it down.

"That is so cool!" Luke dropped in another minnow.

It was extraordinary that Sushi was still alive. No one had expected him to live beyond a few days. Already he'd outlived everyone's predictions, even the experts.

Luke petted Sushi's head as if it were a sacred thing. The power of love, Jessie thought. Just yesterday she'd read an ornithology report about various attempts to raise loons in captivity. Not one loon had survived. Was that because none of them had been loved?

"Because I love there is an invisible way across the sky, birds travel that way..."

She knew from her university psychology classes that when the babies of any species had their custodial needs taken care of, but weren't loved, they had an alarming propensity to die. Why would birds be any different? She thought of what Freud was reported to have said on his death bed. When asked by a colleague to pick the most important thing a psychiatrist could do with clients, his response had surprised everyone. "Love them," he'd said.

In Jessie's experience, lack of love was at the root of many of her clients' ailments, so much so that if she'd had her way, it would be listed as a psychological condition. At least it wasn't one Sushi suffered from. Already he had made a firm nest in their hearts. Almost every day, they telephoned Sushi's progress to Maggie, who warned them not to get their hopes up. Not get their hopes up? Wasn't that like telling balloons not to rise?

"Look, Gran, look!" Holding his nose, Luke dropped under water and spread his legs wide. Sushi darted through. Triumphant, Luke rose like a cork and shook the water off his face. Then he reached for one of Sushi's favourite toys, a blue-haired troll, but Sushi yanked it away.

Jessie didn't know why, but she'd always thought birds were dumb. What's the expression? Birdbrained? Sushi's intelligence took her by surprise. So did the strength of his personality. If they left him alone in the pool for a few minutes, he "told" them in no uncertain terms this wasn't acceptable, making whiney chirping noises until someone joined him. When he wanted to defecate, he paced the side of the pool until someone lifted him out, and, when anyone wanted to play, he picked up the game easily. All this from a bird that had lost both parents and was out of his natural environment.

Jessie finished her tea, and craving some alone time, asked Elfy to keep an eye on Luke and headed down to the dock. The lake was gun grey with a light mist curling on the surface. Bypassing the canoe, she slipped her yellow kayak into the water and paddled along the shore in the opposite direction from Wildwood. She didn't want to think about Dick Price this morning, let alone run into him.

She always felt like a duck when she was in a kayak because of the way the boat sat low in the water and swished its back end quickly from one direction to the other. Dipping the ends of the paddle gently into the liquid silver of the lake, she watched the water spin in little apostrophes. It was well into the morning now, but she imagined she was waking the lake up, stirring it into life.

A loon was calling a few bays over. Was that Sushi's parents? Brother? Sister? The wild, haunting sound tumbled and turned in the mist. It made her heart swell to hear it but filled her with a strange yearning. It was as if the loon were calling to the wilderness within her and to the wilderness within all intelligent life. Calling in a plaintive, intimate way, as one might call to a family member.

It was strange. In the last few weeks, she'd felt as if not only the loons were calling her, but all birds everywhere. It was as if they could feel her concern for them and were attempting to recruit her to fight on their behalf. Hadn't a similar thing happened with trees? The minute she'd shown a willingness to work on their behalf, an awareness of trees moved into her psyche, filling her days and nights with thoughts of them. Then, before she knew it, she had such a case of tree fever that she'd put her life at stake to save some.

Now, the birds seemed to be conscripting her for the same type of devoted service. It was as if the trees had told the birds: go get that Jessie Dearborn. She's a great volunteer. Did she have the option of saying no? Thanks, but no thanks? She didn't feel as if she did, any more than she could have said no to the goose with the arrow in its neck. That's what had started all this. And where was that goose now? Flying high, she hoped.

The wind was gusting up now, and waves were beginning to roll towards her. Jessie turned the kayak around to go back. The loon continued to call, but it sounded more lamenting now, as if it knew its call was destined to go unanswered.

Filled with sadness and a heavy feeling of foreboding, she paddled back. By the time she reached the dock, her body ached with tiredness. All she wanted was to go to sleep. Thinking she would creep back into the house and take a quick nap, she picked up the morning paper and trudged up the wooden steps. She was halfway up when she stopped. Was this what Aggie had been upset about?

There, on the front page was a photograph of Dick Price's desk with a tree stump sitting on top of it. Under it was the caption: "Loon Stumps Price". Jessie swallowed and read the article.

"Someone calling themselves 'The Loon' paid a visit to Wildwood early yesterday, leaving a tree stump on Dick Price's desk. Chained to the trunk was a sign saying, 'Stop Price Now.' Dick Price, the owner of the lodge, is planning a controversial eighteen-hole golf course. When interviewed, Price said he had no idea who would have committed what he called 'such a childish prank'. Police are investigating."

Jessie hobbled up the steps. Was this Elfy's doing? Was she "The Loon"? It was exactly the kind of prank she would delight in playing. Jessie shivered despite the heat of the day and looked at the stump in the photograph again. It was huge. Certainly not something Elfy could have lifted. Besides, Elfy wasn't good at keeping secrets. If she'd pulled off such a prank, she would never have been able to keep quiet about it.

Deciding that she'd ask Elfy about the stump anyway the minute she saw her, she trudged up the steps. The question was, if Elfy wasn't The Loon, who was? She thought back to the council meeting about Dick's dock application. There had been many angry people present. Orf was one. Like hundreds of Muskoka guys, Orf called himself a contractor and picked up jobs fixing docks and building small additions. A large man with a belly that arrived before he did, he had spread himself over the chair beside Jessie and told her he was "none too happy about all of them there boats" that were going to be going past his house if Price's plan went ahead. Every time Price or his lawyer had stood to talk, Orf had belched. But, belching was one thing. Going to the trouble of planting a five hundred-pound tree stump on someone's desk was another.

Jessie didn't like pranks. And anonymous acts made her nervous. There was something dangerous about them. Anonymity had a way of throwing a cloak of impunity around things, giving permission for the darker side of life to come crawling out. It also created an environment in which everything and everyone became suspect.

At the top of the steps, she stood for a moment to get her breath. Goodness, she was tired. She needed a nap, and she needed one soon. She'd think better after that. Near the pool, she noticed Luke and Sushi were gone. Good, she thought. Luke must have taken Sushi inside. That meant she had a chance to get some sleep. She was almost at the door when a car pulled into the driveway. A Jaguar. Who drove a Jaguar? Unable to see through the tinted glass, she limped towards it. Then another car pulled in behind. A police car. She stopped walking. What was going on? And how was she going to find the energy to handle it?

•   •   •

Alex considered making a run for it. As she'd driven north, she'd checked her mirror continually to see if anyone was following her, but no one had been. Until about a mile back. Then a police car had pulled in behind her. Telling herself not to be paranoid, she'd carried on, driving exactly the speed limit. When she'd turned up Jessie's road, the police car had followed. Feeling like an escapee from an asylum, she'd broken into a sweat.

As she pulled into the parking area, the police car pulled in to her right. She waited for the cop to jump out of his car and aim a gun at her like in the movies, but he did no such thing. In fact, he seemed preoccupied with some papers. For a moment, Alex thought about gunning the car and charging back down the road, but didn't. She'd done enough running. Besides, what crime had she committed? Since when was it illegal to visit a friend? Hoisting her best *I'm a lawyer* look to her face, she got out of the car. If she couldn't intimidate a cop, she wasn't worth her law degree.

Jessie looked at her with surprise. "Alex!" The cop got out of his car, and Alex saw Jessie's glance shift over to him. "Hello, Stuart! What brings you here?"

Alex held her breath, waiting for the cop to speak. She could feel the officer studying her face, but then he turned to Jessie.

"I'm on delivery from the sheriff's office," he said. He handed Jessie some papers as if he didn't want anything more to do with them.

Alex let her breath out, then saw the look of distress on Jessie's face.

"It's the eviction—" Jessie stopped and read on.

Something automatic in Alex took over. "Mind if I take a look at that?" The least she could do was check the legality of the forms. The cop stared at her. "Alex Lockhart," she said to him. "I'm a lawyer."

Jessie looked at her numbly but handed over the documents.

"Got papers for Maggie too," he said. "Know how to reach her?"

"Wouldn't tell you if we did, Stu," Elfy said from where she stood in the doorway of the house.

Alex recognized the woman from the hospital visit, and they nodded at each other.

"Hello, Elfy," Stuart said.

Elfy ignored him, turned to Alex. "It legal?"

Alex wasn't an expert in this area of law, but recently she'd helped Tom's nephew with a landlord and tenant problem and had reviewed the basics. From what she could see, the form was a properly executed notice of termination. The landlord, a Mr. Dick Price, stated he was taking back the property for his own use, which was one of the few criteria for legally ending a tenancy. "As far as I can see." She scrutinized it more.

"You can tell that bastard we're not budging!" Elfy said.

Jessie leaned against the car. "Maybe we should go and talk to him."

Elfy swatted the air. "Think that turkey's going to listen?"

"Don't go without your lawyer," Alex warned.

"Waste of time if you ask me," Elfy said.

Jessie stuffed the papers into her pocket. "I'm sorry, Alex, I'm not giving you a very warm welcome."

"It's all right," Alex said. "This looks like something you have to deal with. Want me to come along to talk to this guy? Give you some legal back-up?"

"Would you?" Jessie asked, relief on her face.

Alex followed Jessie and the two of them got into the tin boat. Alex sat in the bow and Jessie steered them out into the choppy water. Waves slapped against the side of the boat.

"Thanks for this," Jessie said.

They were sitting close, facing each other. "No problem," Alex said, feeling awkward.

"It's probably an exercise in futility." Jessie shrugged. "Sorry this had to happen the moment you arrived."

"No, it's fine. I shouldn't have just landed on you." Alex looked away and gazed out on to the lake. She could feel Jessie's eyes *reading* her, interpreting her, and felt a moment's panic. Maybe it had been a mistake to come. Jessie was going to ask questions, want to *talk*. What could she say? My husband and father were trying to have me committed so I took off?

"Alex, is everything all right?"

"I—I needed to get away. That's all."

Jessie nodded. "I know the feeling."

An empty space settled between them. In it wafted Lucy's ghost.

"Stay as long as you like," Jessie said.

Alex didn't know what to say. She, who always knew what to say. Jessie was going to think she was an absolute idiot.

"Trade you lodging for legal advice," Jessie said. "Looks like we're going to need plenty of that."

Alex swallowed and looked away. She felt a lump in her throat, and, not trusting herself to speak, looked around the lake. The landscape reminded her of Camp Ahmanee. How Tom would like this, she thought. Did Tom ever think of the camp any more? Did he ever yearn to get away? If he did, no one would ever know. He hadn't been out of the city in years.

Ahead, Alex could see a quaint, old-fashioned lodge. Was this where this man Price lived? She wouldn't have imagined he'd live in a place of such charm. Then, realizing they would soon be there, she brought her attention back to Jessie. "You'd better tell me the history of this dispute. So I'm up to speed."

Jessie gave the barest of facts and was just finishing her explanation when they reached the lodge. There were several teenagers sprawled on the dock. None of them moved.

"Is your father in?" Jessie asked a boy with spiked orange hair. He had on almond-shaped mirrored sunglasses. Alex couldn't see his eyes.

"Who wants to know?"

Alex stepped over the boy's legs. "We'll find him."

•   •   •

Jessie felt DJ's eyes on her back as she walked up the stone pathway to the lodge. She hadn't liked the way he'd sneered at her. She pulled her thoughts away from him and tried to think about what she was going to say to the boy's father. They passed the tall totem pole, and one of the faces frowned at her as if in warning.

"That normal?" Alex asked, nodding towards the security guard who was watching them approach.

Jessie shook her head. It must be a result of the tree stump incident, she thought, making a mental note to tell Alex about that later. They climbed the log steps and walked across the wide, wooden verandah where guests sat out at night playing cards or dancing. Memories paraded across her mind. There, in the corner, on that wooden love seat, was where she'd first kissed her husband. Once upon another time.

Over the main door there was a red wooden sign with the word "Wildwood" carved into it. That sign had been there as long as Jessie had known the lodge. Inside, they went to the office where Alex informed the receptionist she was a lawyer and wanted to see Mr. Price.

The receptionist eyed them nervously, then picked up the phone. "Can I ask the nature of the matter?"

"No, you may not," Alex said calmly and sat down in one of the wicker chairs.

Jessie smiled at the authority Alex exuded. All that was missing was the "super-lawyer" cape. And to think she'd been bothered by Alex's control patterns.

Red-haired and freckled, Dick Price ushered them into the office as if he'd been expecting them. As introductions were made, Jessie looked around. There were no family photos on the walls or on his desk, but there was something on a table next to Price's desk that caught her eye. It was a miniature model of some sort of amusement park. She could see a carnival area with rides, and there was a shooting range and tennis courts. In the centre was a large hotel-type building made mostly of glass which overlooked the first hole of the full-sized, eighteen-hole golf course. At the edge of the golf course were dozens of trails zig-zagging through the woods. On the paved pathways, there were little miniaturized bumper cars. Was this the prototype of some sort of theme park he was involved in? She'd heard that Price had worked for one in the States before coming here. The one on his table looked like something that belonged in Florida or California.

It was the kind of place she hated. She'd never been to a theme park in her life and didn't ever want to visit one. To her, they were the fast food of the leisure world. Thankfully, they weren't big in Canada. Yet.

Then she saw the red wooden plaque over the glass door of the model. "This—this is Wildwood?"

Dick Price rocked back in his plum-coloured leather chair. He viewed the model proudly. "Unrecognizable, isn't it? We're going to renovate from stem to stern. Give it a complete facelift."

She saw her arm fling out, wipe the entire model off

the table, but sat still, feeling sick. "But the building."

"Nothing but a fire trap the way it is now," he said. "Besides, with the golf course, we're going to need more rooms. We expect to have over a hundred people on any given night. Do you golf, Ms. Lockhart?"

Alex said nothing. Dick Price carried on.

"As you can imagine, an overhaul of this magnitude means other things have to go. My two rental houses have to be torn down..."

Jessie opened her mouth to speak, but no words came.

"Or we wouldn't have an eighteenth hole on the golf course. And we wouldn't want that, would we?"

Alex cleared her throat. "Mr. Price, I understand there were rental agreements made by the previous owner."

"Nothing in writing."

Jessie found her voice, and it came out booming. "Archie gave his word!"

Price kept his eyes on Alex. "You're a lawyer. You know the law. Unless you have some sort of written contract to the contrary, I have the right to terminate, and I'm going to terminate." He crossed his arms in front of his chest.

Alex carried on. "Are you open to negotiation?"

Price turned to look directly at Jessie. His eyes were hard. "I don't negotiate with radicals. People who put tree stumps—"

"That wasn't me!"

The loudness of Price's voice squashed Jessie's. "And just in case you're thinking about any other *pranks*—" He turned back to Alex. "You can tell your client that I now have a security system in place. Twenty-four hours a day. Anyone caught on the property after hours will be arrested on sight."

He stood up and handed Alex a card. "If there are any further questions, I suggest you contact my lawyer."

•   •   •

When Jessie showed her where she'd be staying, Alex could hardly believe her good fortune. It was a living area all to itself in the bottom part of the house, wood-panelled, with bookcases everywhere. The bedroom was tiny, but had a large window with a pine tree so close the green fronds brushed against the glass. The bed was covered with a hand-made quilt and had a nest-like depression in the centre.

If questions were going to come, they were going to come now, Alex thought, and steeled herself, but Jessie, obviously preoccupied with the meeting they'd just had with Price, muttered something about having to think and went off.

Alex walked through the rooms. Most places she'd lived in her life had definite personalities. They "made a statement" as one of her designers once phrased it. If this place said anything, it was "Let yourself be." She wandered out to the little deck off the kitchen. In the middle of it was a single chair facing the lake. She sat down and the chair pulled her back into it. At the hospital, craziness had seemed so close, stalking her like a bogey man, ready to pounce. Even when she was staying in the coach house, the craziness lurked. But here, the lush trees and expansive lake brought her peace.

But what about Tom? And her children? She'd left them. *Run.* She reined in her thoughts. No, she was going to think of it in another way: that she was taking a break, having a short holiday. Normal people took holidays all the time. Why shouldn't she? Everyone needed time off. She'd give herself a few days to gather her resources, then throw herself back into the ring.

Having assuaged her guilt with this decision, she made herself think about Jessie's eviction notice. No matter what angle she approached it from, she couldn't think of a way to fight it. The law was the law, and Price had the full weight of it on his side. Too bad, she thought. This was a lovely place. But you couldn't stop progress. And you couldn't stop men like Price. She'd met so many men like him over the years, men who were used to money and power and getting their way. She sighed. Twice she'd caught him looking at her breasts. Sex and money. They fuelled everything.

Still, she wasn't going to give up without talking to some of her colleagues who specialized in landlord and tenant law. As she sorted through the possibilities, the sun grew hotter and her eyes began to close. In the city, sleeping had never been easy. She begrudged the hours that sleep took away from work and never went to bed until she was exhausted. Days would pass without her feeling rested. But now, with the soothing sound of lake water lapping, she couldn't help herself and fell into sleep like a patient might collapse into the arms of a nurse, with open-armed, body-slack surrender.

Chapter 9

Something was wrong with Sushi.

"Look," Luke said. The loon was pecking and pecking at his skin.

No, Jessie thought. Not another bad thing. First there was her foot. Then the eviction notice and the golf course. How could more go wrong? Were they jinxed? She felt beyond her ability to cope. Out on the lake, the sound of the jet-ski droned on. DJ had been out there for hours.

She looked down at Sushi as he pecked himself. She didn't know what to make of it. She cursed and flipped a tape into the tape player. Sometimes music settled him down. The lamenting voice of Neil Young filled the room. *Comes a time...*

"Hey, Sush, your favourite song." She lifted Sushi into her arms and walked with him like she might a small baby. Usually Sushi found Neil's voice soothing, but not today. He continued to peck compulsively at his skin. They'd been warned he would get sick. Warned by everyone. Was he going to die? *Don't go there,* she told herself. But this was bad, there was no denying it.

"Where the heck is Harley?"

Luke shrugged. He looked worried, and not wanting to see his worry, Jessie told him to go outside. There was nothing he could do anyway. He didn't move.

"GO!"

What was the matter with kids these days? Couldn't they do what they were told? She watched Luke walk away, his head down, and she felt awful. Why was it that one bad thing seemed to lead to another? She set Sushi down and rummaged through some homeopathic remedies Maggie had left, wondering which one to use. It was hard to figure out a remedy when she didn't know what was wrong, but she chose one for stress.

Then she flipped on another tape and turned the volume up. The sound of water lapping and loons calling filled the room. She shook her head. What was the world coming to that she had to go to a store to buy a tape to hear the sounds she should be hearing outside her door! But she had to drown out the sound of the jet-ski. She couldn't stand it anymore. It grated like a dentist's drill. Indignation boiled up inside her, pressing against her skin, making it prickle. She felt hot and sick and agitated. She made herself breathe and began to pace. *It's all right*, she told herself. *It's all right.* She paced and breathed, but DJ's face kept appearing.

Fuck you.

Fuck you.

What right had he to talk to her like that? She hadn't been rude to him. Now she wished she had been rude. She imagined herself screaming at him.

As a child, she used to like seeing licence plates from different places: New York, Pennsylvania, Michigan. It had made her proud to know that people from far and wide wanted to come to Muskoka. She understood their need to get away from the noise and craziness of the city. When she'd lived in the city, she'd felt the same way. She remembered how great it had been to leave the urban sprawl and come to Muskoka, where she could rejuvenate with a bit of wilderness.

Unfortunately, the kind of tourist that had been coming to Muskoka lately wasn't interested in wilderness. Not real wilderness. The wilderness they wanted was the loon on the sign going into the cottage or a few birds on the feeder by the hot tub. Designer wilderness.

Jessie looked out on the lake and began counting boats. Including DJ's, she could see fifteen. Fifteen! Grand Central Station, or what? She let her eyes move along the shoreline. Once upon a time, there had been only a handful of cottages in this bay, but now the shoreline was littered with huge, multi-million dollar mansions. Some even had swimming pools. Swimming pools! What was wrong with the water in the lake? People didn't come to Muskoka for nature, they came to *use* it, like some sort of geographical bimbo.

And the town politicians seemed only too happy to sell the place to the highest bidder! Recently, the town council had spent thousands of dollars painting Muskoka scenes on the side of transport trucks that travelled down to the States. At the bottom of the painting, it said "Muskoka" and a phone number. Sure, make Muskoka a pin-up girl. Why didn't they add: "For a good time, call Muskoka."

In front of her, DJ raced his purple plastic boat with the yellow flames around the buoy that marked some rocks a few hundred feet out. She shook her head. *Go on, bash right into them!* It would serve him right.

When she was a kid, there hadn't been buoys on the lake. Back then, people were expected to know the water, know where the rocks and shallow places were. People respected the lake and got to know it. If they hit a rock, it was just too bad. A lesson learned. Maybe if DJ hit the rocks now, it would teach him some respect.

The noise from the jet-ski became bigger and louder, then bigger and louder still. He became the epitome of all she was powerless to stop. And in her fury, an idea slithered out from a crevice in her mind. All anyone would have to do was move the buoy a few feet and it would no longer mark where the rocks were. A boat going as close as DJ's would hit them for sure. Which would put his boat out of commission. By the time he got his boat fixed, the summer would be almost over. Meanwhile, they would have a few weeks of peace and quiet.

It was an evil thought. The kind one has, then discards. But she couldn't discard it. In an attempt to dislodge it, she brought the force of her logic to bear against it. Such an act would be illegal. And potentially dangerous. It would also be impossible. There was no way a person could move a buoy for just a few minutes. This last thought relieved her. She was glad the idea couldn't work. She forgave herself for having it. It was just that when someone spit in your face, it was hard not to want to lift your hand and wipe it away.

Luke hurried in with Harley and Elfy behind.

"It's like he's got ants in his pants," Elfy said, eyeing Sushi worriedly. "See?" Luke said. Jessie put her arm around the boy's shoulders and pulled him close. She was glad that he let her.

Harley took Sushi gently from Jessie and looked at him closely.

"Think we should call that guy in the States again?" Elfy asked. "Not that the creep knew anything when we first called him."

But Harley was smiling. "Feathers," he said.

Jessie looked from Harley to Sushi. Feathers, what did he mean, feathers? Sushi was nothing *but* feathers. She studied the bird more closely. Up until now, Sushi had been covered with a soft fuzzy down, but when she looked at his skin, she could see the tips of something trying to break through. Were those his new feathers?

Elfy got it first. "He's molting! Well, I'll be darned!"

"Must hurt," Luke said.

"Like a baby teething," Jessie said. She was relieved, then remembered what Maggie had said about molting. Of all the stages of a bird's development, molting was the most stressful. Sushi had already had more stress than any loon alive. Would he be able to handle more?

Elfy was thinking the same way. "We're going to have to keep all the other stresses to a minimum for a few days. Till he gets through this."

Whack. Whack. Whack.

In unison, they turned to watch the jet-ski.

"Not much chance of that," Harley said.

Elfy shook her head. "Should be a law, eh?" She frowned. "Jake Corbett told me he tried talking to the kid. And Jake's no pushover. Told me it was like walking into a sewer. *It's a free world man, and I can do what I frigging well want.*"

Jessie nodded. From the sound of it, Jake had been told to "fuck off" too.

"Hey, Harls," Elfy said, "how about cleaning that gun of yours down on the dock. Have it accidentally shoot someone's head off."

Harley smiled, but his body was still, very still.

"They'd send you away for ten years," Elfy said, "but—"

"Ten? With my blood, it would be twenty!"

Elfy shrugged. "Yeah, but think of the peace and quiet. Eh, Jess? Wouldn't you just kill for some of that?"

"Yes, I believe I would," Jessie said. It was at that exact moment that the idea of how to move the buoy dropped into her mind. It landed like a grenade into a pond. She shook her head as if to flick off the water. It was so simple, so simple it was frightening. But as she told clients: sometimes it was difficult to tell the difference between fear and excitement.

• • •

The Grannies arrived at the house like they were coming to a party. As Jessie finished her foot exercises, she watched Aggie hurry up the driveway. For someone with arthritis in her knees, Aggie was moving at quite a clip.

"Yoo-hoo!" Aggie called.

Jessie pulled her foot out of the water, called to Luke to cover for her with Sushi and went to greet her.

"I'm early, I know." She brushed Jessie's cheek with hers.

"You're always early." They walked towards the house. Jessie felt small beside Aggie's opulent body.

"I was even born early. My mother was at the opera when she went into labour. I was born backstage as Maria Callas sang *Carmen*."

"You just couldn't wait to get down here and start organizing everyone."

A smile wriggled on Aggie's mouth. "Pretty much."

Jessie put the water on for tea and went to change. When she came back into the living room, Aggie was standing formidably at the front of the room like a general about to command her troops. Estelle and Joey were just arriving.

Estelle, tall and thin, picked her way through the furniture like a heron through reeds. "How exciting," she said to everyone in her low, macabre voice.

Joey threw her arms around Jessie.

Jessie squeezed Joey's rotund body. The steroids Joey had to take to control her asthma made her body look like an over-inflated beach ball.

"Yo! Elf!" Joey thrust her arm into the air as Elfy came in with Grace. Jessie looked at Grace to see if she was all right. Diagnosed with bowel cancer the year before, Grace had undergone surgery, and, although the doctors had said they had gotten it all, Grace did not look well. But despite her pale face, she was smiling brightly. Joey leaned over and kissed her, then exchanged a high five with Elfy.

Jessie settled herself into a chair. It saddened her to see how much everyone had aged. Like a marching band, the life force that had made these women loud as trumpets when they'd banded together to save some trees a few years ago had now paraded past them, leaving an unquiet silence.

"How's your new hip?" Elfy asked Estelle.

Estelle swivelled slowly like she was twirling a hula-hoop. She'd recently had her second hip replacement.

"Hubba, hubba!" Joey said, pulling a bag of cookies from her purse. She took three and passed the bag around. "Next thing you know you'll be joining Aggie's belly-dancing class."

Grace wrinkled her brow. "Belly-dancing, Agatha?"

Indignant, Aggie opened her mouth to speak, but Elfy beat her to it.

"She had to drop out. They couldn't find a gem big enough for her belly button."

Aggie rolled her eyes.

"Yee-ha!" Joey thumped her fists on her huge thighs. "The Grannies ride again!"

Wearing a T-shirt that said "Aged To Perfection", Elfy stood up and faced the group.

"All right, you guys, we all know how serious this is. There's a lot more than a few beautiful trees at stake this time, there's Wildwood itself, Jessie's place here, and, if that doesn't get your knickers in a knot, the bird refuge."

Aggie, never comfortable giving up leadership for long, cleared her throat. "At least we know what to do. I'll book the community hall."

Elfy's hand leapt to her head. "We did that last time!"

Aggie glanced at Elfy like she might a dust ball under the bed. "We did that last time, and it worked!"

"What *worked* was us getting down and dirty," Elfy said, "and the mayor knew it."

Aggie straightened her back. "Nonsense. We won because we had a community meeting and rallied support!"

Jessie sighed. "Come on, you two. Don't start." They had bickered like this throughout the tree campaign.

"We can't ask people to fight if they don't know the issues," Estelle said.

Aggie nodded. "Exactly!"

Joey looked nervously at Elfy. "It's no big deal to do a community meeting..." She put an entire cookie in her mouth.

"I can do the flyer," Estelle said.

"I'll hand some out," Grace said.

"Good," Aggie said. "I'll book the community centre then."
She took out a note pad from her purse. "I'm also going to
inquire about the possibility of having Wildwood designated an
historical site. I'll call Bernard and see what he thinks."

"Who's Bernard?" Grace whispered.

"Aggie's boyfriend," Estelle whispered back. "A
lawyer."

"*Was* a lawyer," Elfy said loudly.

Aggie sniffed. "Just because he's retired from his law
practice doesn't make him less of a lawyer. He's still got
valuable connections."

"Glad he's got something," Elfy said.

"More than the man in *your* life," Aggie said.

Elfy frowned. "You two do it?"

Aggie grit her teeth. Elfy carried on.

"You know. The jiggy-jiggy…the bump and grind…"

"Elfy, don't be so naughty," Estelle said.

"Want to hear a joke?" Elfy didn't wait for an answer.
"Schwarzenegger has a big one, Michael J. Fox has a small
one, Madonna doesn't have one at all and the Pope never
uses his. What is it?"

They all waited for the punch line.

"I'll bite," Joey said and smirked.

"What!" Grace said.

"A last name!"

"You had me, Elf, you had me." Joey's belly jiggled
with laughter. The others groaned.

"*That* was a joke?" Aggie pulled the group back on
topic, directing the discussion to press releases, petitions
and a letter campaign.

"Been there! Done that! Got the T-shirt!" Elfy cried.
"Come on, we need to wake people up, shake things up."

Jessie shifted in her seat.

"What you got in mind, Elf?" Joey asked.

"Nothing that dynamite tied to Price's dick, sorry, dock, wouldn't fix." Her laugh sounded loud in the quiet room.

"Wasn't putting that tree stump on his desk enough?" Aggie said.

Elfy smiled. "You think I'm The Loon? Ha! I'll take that as a compliment."

Aggie pounced. "You would."

"Hope it wasn't The Loon that put bird shit on my car," Joey said.

"I had that too. All over my windshield," Estelle said.

Jessie tensed. She didn't like the sound of this. Pranks had a way of leading to other pranks, and each round tended to up the stakes.

"We should put bird shit on that Lincoln of Price's," Joey said. "See how *he* likes it."

"I didn't have any on my car," Grace said.

Joey looked at her softly. "Grace, you don't have a car."

Grace's eyebrows pressed together as if trying to squeeze a memory out of her brain. "No, I guess I...don't."

Elfy shook her head. "Wake up, you guys. The frigging planet is hurtling towards destruction and all you're doing is flapping your jaws about it."

Aggie rolled her eyes. "We're not talking about the world, Elfy, we're talking about Wildwood."

"Wildwood *is* my world," Elfy said. "We've got to get people's attention. Get them to realize—"

Aggie raised her chest. "I won't do anything that isn't legal."

Jessie frowned. She'd been thinking a lot lately about the word "legal". Normally, she thought of herself as a fairly law-abiding individual. But what was a person to do when the laws weren't fair? Or simply weren't in place yet, as was the case with many environmental concerns. Should she simply stand by while the birds and animals, even her beloved lake, were destroyed? She wouldn't be able to live with herself! No, first and foremost, was her moral obligation to the wild things she loved! Even if that meant breaking the law!

During the campaign to save the trees, she'd broken the law. She'd chained herself to a tree trunk and stopped the destruction of a small forest. Even now, she knew that had been the right thing to do. After all, what were laws but a group of guidelines to govern the behaviour people thought necessary at a given time? Laws weren't always right or just. A hundred years ago it had been legal to beat women and own slaves. History was full of people who broke laws and changed the world for the better.

"Legal-smeegle," Elfy said, forcing Jessie's attention back to the meeting. Elfy tucked her curled hands up into her armpits to mimic wings. She flapped them back and forth like a chicken.

"Elfreda!" Estelle said and turned to Aggie. "Think about Gandhi. He changed the world yet stayed within the law."

"Gandhi—he the guy that did that hunger strike?" Joey sounded alarmed.

"You going on a hunger strike?" Grace asked.

"I'd blow up a building easier than I'd give up food," Joey said.

Aggie looked at Jessie. "Don't you think Elfy's going a

little far? Acting a tad radical?"

Elfy added squawking noises to her chicken imitation.

"Stop it!" Aggie shouted. Everyone was silent.

Grace turned to Jessie and asked in a small voice, "What do you think?"

Jessie sighed. "I don't know. Sometimes I don't know which is crazier—getting radical or not getting radical." Besides, how did one define radical, anyway? She thought about one of her clients, Sarah Childs, who'd been beaten by her father. By the time Sarah was an adult, she was so used to abuse that when her husband began pushing her around, she did nothing to stop it. When Jessie suggested she say "no", this felt radical to the woman.

Wasn't that similar to what was happening with the environment? Everyone was so used to the pollution and ecological atrocities, it felt radical to demand something else. But what was so radical about clean air? Or clean water? She knew the statistics. Although Canadians were always imagining the U.S. had more pollution, Canadians put far more toxic chemicals into the air than their southern neighbour and ended up killing forty people prematurely every day from poisoned air.

Sometimes when she thought about her grandchildren and her grandchildren's children, she imagined them asking her, not why her generation had been so radical about saving the environment, but why her generation hadn't been more radical.

"Look," Joey said. "Doing *something* is better than doing *nothing*. Let's start with the community meeting, see how much support we get, and then, if we need to do more, we will."

Everyone looked at Elfy.

"Come on, Elfy," Joey said. "Say okay, so we can order pizza."

Elfy pressed her thin lips together, but nodded.

Joey whistled and thrust her plump arm out for the phone.

• • •

Alex lay in bed as a gang of thoughts worked her over. She turned from side to side, trying to escape, but they came after her. *Are you crazy? Have you left your senses? You're wrecking everything. Everything you've built. Go back right now. Before your father hires someone else.*

Startled, she sat up in bed. Would her father do that? Hire someone else? She'd never considered this a possibility before, but now she realized that was exactly what her father would do if she didn't go back right away. Every day she'd told herself she would call him, explain that she was coming back in a few weeks, but every day she didn't make the call. Fear trickled down her spine. Was it too late? Should she run upstairs and call him now? Yes, that's exactly what she should do. So, why was she sitting here?

Look, you can't spend the rest of your life not working. And, if you have to work, you'll never find a boss better than your father. Call him now!

Shaken, she went into the small kitchen. She needed a cup of coffee first. Damn. There was no milk. On the window sill was a card from Lucy's family. The card was a reply to a letter Jessie had written. Jessie had thought Alex might like to see it, but Alex hadn't even opened it. She was waiting until she had more of a grip. As she thought about Lucy, the craziness swung close again. Like a House of Horrors monster, it lunged towards her as if from out of nowhere.

Her palms began to sweat. She definitely needed a coffee. She told herself she could go upstairs to get milk from Jessie's kitchen, but couldn't get herself to do it. The bird room was beside the kitchen and the thought of being near anything sick repelled her. So far, she'd kept her distance from the baby loon too, which wasn't easy, because it was adorable with its big webbed feet and fluffy body. But the loon wasn't supposed to live either, so she stayed away.

Deciding to have her coffee black, she put the kettle on the stove and paced while she waited for it to boil. She was worried about Evan. When she'd talked to Tom yesterday, he'd told her Evan's school had to augment his asthma medicine after she'd left. Alex felt her insides twist. Her child, her son, needed her and here she was, lollygagging around a cottage, having a holiday. She was going to have to put a stop to this self-indulgent silliness and go back. She could pack up her things and leave this morning if she wanted. Be back at the office by mid-afternoon.

She missed Evan awfully. Every time she talked to him, he begged her to let him visit. She knew part of that was because of Sushi. Ever since she'd told him about Luke and the loon, he'd pestered her with questions. The only way she'd been able to put him off was by telling him she was coming home.

The poor boy. He missed her. Unlike Christina, who hadn't called once. The only time Alex had talked to her was when she'd specifically asked Tom to put her on the phone. During the conversation Christina had been cool, full of teenage disinterest.

From her father, she had heard nothing. Once before, when she'd announced she was getting married, he'd given her the silent treatment like this, but even then, it hadn't lasted. After a few days, they'd patched things up. Could they still patch things up now, or was it too late? The only way to find out was to call him.

Pick up the phone! a voice inside her screamed.

Her hand remained immobile.

Truly anxious now, she went outside. It was early, and the sun was breaking through the mist and making long, white columns through the trees. It was so beautiful here. Too bad it all had to change. Would this very spot be the sixth hole on the golf course? The tenth? She imagined all the trees gone and a fairway in front of her congested with golf carts. According to reports, Price was going to spend millions. Lucky him to have that kind of money.

She thought about the "Save Wildwood" campaign Jessie and the others were trying to launch. A valiant effort, she thought, but a total waste of time. As always, the highest bidder would win, and it was obvious who that was going to be. Now, if Jessie had money, the situation would be different. Jessie could be a player. *See,* a voice inside her said. *Money rules the world. Without money, you just get pushed around.*

Alex wandered down towards the dock hoping the serenity of the lake would calm her. She felt eyes on her.

"Harley—" He was sitting against a tree near the water, his brown clothes and skin blending into the bark so well he looked like part of the tree. It bothered her to be seen by a man when she felt weak like this. In the money world, she'd learned to stay one up and never show vulnerability. A burst of sunlight brightened the air. She looked at Harley, expecting to see that self-satisfied dominant look men were so good at, but his eyes offered only ease.

"How are you?" he asked.

"Had a rough night," she said, then realized he could see this. *Stupid,* she hissed at herself. But Harley's face was kind, and she found herself opening to him, like she might open her jacket on a warm day.

"Want to talk?"

How could she talk to a man like Harley? The man had a *ponytail,* for God's sake! But she found herself talking to him, despite herself, telling him about Lucy and about the psychiatrist, then about her dilemma with her father.

"If I was using my head, I'd go in and call my father right now," she said.

Harley tapped his forehead with his finger. "Your head doesn't know everything." He looked at her seriously. "Sometimes, it just can't get you where you want to go." Abruptly, he stood up and motioned her to follow.

Seeing him set off up the path, she called, "Where are you going?"

Harley stepped into the density of trees. For such a big man, he moved with a silent lightness. But he moved swiftly, too, and she realized she'd lose him if she didn't follow. The voice of her urban education told her she'd be a fool to follow a man she hardly knew into the woods. Besides, what she needed to do was go back inside and call her father. Charlie bounded ahead of her, his tail swishing and, as if her body had a mind of its own, she went after them.

Twigs snapped beneath her feet, and she could smell the lushness of green things as she stepped through the dappled light. Ahead of her, Harley walked soundlessly, leading her along a stream, then up a huge sloping rock. The trees became thicker and the light dimmer. She wanted to turn back, but knew she'd never find her way. When they came to an open place, Harley stopped and Charlie sat on his haunches beside him. Spread in front of them was an immense bed of emerald green moss. Harley put his palms on the moss and Alex did the same. It felt spongy and alive.

Harley motioned her to lie down. Alex looked at him sharply. He was so close, she could smell the woody maleness of him. For all she knew, he might molest her. Even rape her. But there was nothing predatory in Harley's face, only serene amusement. Feeling flustered that he might know what she'd been thinking, she lay down self-consciously. The trees stretched above her like long poles, and she could see their leafy tops swaying slightly in the breeze. She closed her eyes. The earthy smell of the moss rose up from the ground all around her. When she opened her eyes, Harley was gone.

Great. Now what was she going to do? She was stuck here until he came back. Whenever that was going to be. Her chances of getting to the city were diminishing by the moment. Knowing there was nothing to be done, she let herself sink into the moss. It felt as if the earth were pulling her down into itself. As it pulled, the muscles in her back slackened and the tension in her body released. The phrase "Mother Earth" passed through her mind. She felt small, like a baby lying on a soft, rounded belly. In a strange, unexplainable way, she felt a presence. *Mother*

Earth, she thought. Tears came to her eyes again. It was as if the earth were trying to pull them out of her, but she willed them back. She would *not* cry. Not now. Not ever.

Charlie stretched his flaxen body and rolled on his back. She rubbed his silky tummy and listened to the wind soughing through the leaves. Birds flitted here and there, a robin perched on a nearby branch and sang, as if to her. She thought of the life she'd had in the city, the cigarettes, the eighteen-hour days, the run, run, running. Just thinking about it tired her. Maybe it hadn't been so crazy to leave that for a little while. Maybe it was the sanest thing she'd ever done.

Chapter 10

Jessie taped a "Save Wildwood" flyer to the glass door of Reader's World, the bookstore, and carried on down the main street, putting up posters wherever she could. Estelle had done this a week ago, but someone had taken all the flyers down. Who? Obviously someone who did not want the meeting to happen. As she walked, she had a funny feeling on her back. It was as if there was a spider crawling on it. Was she being watched?

She caught her eyes scanning the roof of The Factory Store across the street. What was she looking for? A gunman? *Calm down, woman.* Why did she keep imagining something bad was going to happen? She knew why. Because The Loon had struck again.

At least, Price was saying it was The Loon. There had been no identifying note this time. But then, it would have been difficult to pin a note on a few dozen mice. How they'd been set loose in the dining room at Wildwood was anyone's guess. And at the height of the dinner hour too. Of course, pandemonium had broken loose as guests jumped on chairs and screamed. Someone sounded the fire alarm, and soon there were sirens and fire trucks and even more chaos. Gossip had been flying around the town about it for days.

Elfy laughed herself silly when she heard.

Jessie was more cautious. "Someone could have been hurt," she said. "What about that man who had to be taken to the hospital?"

"The guy was ninety-two. And he's fine, or so I've heard. It's the security guard I feel sorry for. Getting the sack like that."

"And now Price has hired two others—"

"He's going to need two *dozen* to stop The Loon."

"There's no proof The Loon did the mice."

Elfy chuckled. "I'd sure like to shake his or her hand."

That was the problem. Anything that went wrong anywhere was now being blamed on The Loon. And although no one knew who The Loon was, everyone was suspecting everyone else. Except for Price, who seemed bent on the idea that Jessie was The Loon. Which wouldn't have bothered her if she hadn't been worried about retaliation.

Making her way quickly along the main street of town, she posted a flyer in The Dollar Store, then crossed over to Armstrong's Variety. In the window of Shards and Shavings, one of the craft stores, she saw a "Save Sushi" banner. Support for the campaign was building every day. It helped that they were getting lots of press. They could thank Aggie for that. Sushi could not have a better press agent.

"Hey, Jesse! How's Sushi?"

Jessie looked across the street. She didn't recognize the person who had called out. This was happening a lot lately, strangers knowing about Sushi, or her or The Grannies. It was good for the campaign that people were becoming aware of what was going on, but it made her feel exposed.

"Still going strong," she shouted. Looking up at the clock tower, she realized she had less time than she thought and had to keep moving. At the end of the stores now, she went into the Tourist Information Office, then zipped back to the restaurant behind it for a cappuccino to go. While the waitress prepared it, she went outside and stood with her arms on the railing of the balcony.

Twenty feet down, the river slid by like a sled on a toboggan run. A few hundred yards downstream, she could see a series of bridges crossing the river, one for the train, another for cars and a third for pedestrians. She wondered what the river would have looked like before all the metal and steel had been constructed over it. And under it too, she thought, remembering the various underwater gates of the town's electricity plant.

Most people liked to look at the water further downstream, where it tumbled over the falls and was all white and frothy, but she liked to see it here, where it was still black and wild and fast.

Feeling someone at her side, she turned and saw the waitress, a take-out cappuccino in hand. Jessie sipped it as she walked back up the main street. Thinking that she'd put a flyer in the window of Scott's, another bookstore, she started to cross the street.

"Hey, bird woman!"

Jessie looked up. Martha stood in the doorway of the newspaper office.

"Hey, ink woman!" she called back. The ongoing miracle of Sushi's survival had captured Martha's interest, and as the editor of the summer paper, she'd been writing a detailed report of Sushi's progress each week. When Sushi had gone through his molt a while back, she'd given her readers a photographic account of his development. And, of course, now that things were heating up between Price and The Loon and The Grannies, there was even more interest from her readers.

"Got something for you," Martha said, handing Jessie a large manilla envelope. "Sushi's fan mail. He's becoming a celebrity."

"Listen, Martha, thanks for all—"

"Thank the readers," she said. "They're the ones who can't get enough of Sushi."

Checking her watch and realizing how far behind she was, Jessie waved and rushed through the little park on the main street to her car. Bordering the park was a group of maples, and she could see some ravens shuffling like a deck of cards in and out of the branches. Then she heard some sparrows. And saw a robin. Birds, they were everywhere, taking over her house, her dreams, her thoughts. Even her clients were beginning to notice. Yesterday, one of them had turned to her and said, "Jessie, are you with me?" And, of course, she hadn't been. She'd been watching the sky.

She was going to have to be more careful. Compartmentalize better. And run faster, she thought, realizing she was almost late for another client. She crossed the road and jogged the last few hundred yards to the car.

Yanking open the door quickly, she hopped into her car and gagged. The stench in the car was vile, suffocating, and she pushed open the door again and gasped for air. It was all she could do not to throw up. As soon as she got a breath, she tumbled from the car and stood with her hand on her chest, leaning against the car. When she opened her eyes, she could see the blood. Red gashes of it, all over the seats. But there were clumps too, grey, almost furry. Then she saw the tails. They were mice, vivisected mice that someone had brutally torn apart and thrown into her car.

Breathing through her mouth, she opened all the doors, then went to the closest restaurant and pulled some paper towels from the dispenser in the washroom. By the time she got back, the noxious smell had dispersed a little and, wrapping some of the towelling around her hand, she picked up the mice by the tails and deposited them in the bin at the end of the parking lot. Then she began wiping the seat off. Who had done this? DJ?

When she had cleaned things as best she could, she went back to the restaurant and washed her hands. Back at the car, the stench was still there, but not as strong and she was able to get back in. Warily, as if expecting something to explode, she turned the key in the ignition. She sat for a few minutes and made herself breathe.

•　•　•

Alex sat on the deck drinking her morning coffee. It didn't taste as good without a cigarette. She knew she could go inside and light up one of the Virginia Slims left in the pack she'd chain-smoked on the way up, but she wouldn't let herself. She'd already told Evan she'd quit, and when he and the rest of the family came to visit in a few days, she didn't want to tell him otherwise. She knew how disappointed he was that she wasn't at home and couldn't stand the idea of letting him down about something else.

Although she was looking forward to seeing them all, she was nervous. It felt different being her these days. Would her family like this version of who she was? A few nights ago, she dreamed she was wandering around the streets in her underwear. Jessie suggested this might mean she was willing to show more of herself, let people see her without her "costume". Was this true? With no one requiring her to put a face on, she hadn't bothered with makeup since she'd arrived here. Except for her family, no one had seen her without makeup since she was twelve. But no one seemed to notice here. What a relief it was not to do face patrol!

She certainly was letting her hair down. Last night, when a favourite song came on the radio, she'd waltzed herself around her living room. And she'd started making collages out of pine cones and pieces of drift wood and anything else she found of interest on her long walks. It was freeing being this new person, but where was it going to lead?

"Trust yourself," Harley kept telling her.

Trust herself? "How do I know I'm not going to end up on a park bench with a bunch of bags all around me?"

Harley had smiled in his amused way, and that had settled her down, but she still felt vulnerable. She'd even confessed that to Jessie one day.

"There's nothing wrong with vulnerability," Jessie had told her. "In fact, it goes along with authenticity."

Alex hadn't stuck around for more analysis. She had to be careful with Jessie. Never had she met anyone so committed to *feelings*. Alex didn't want *feelings*. Talking about feelings might be helpful for some people, but not for her. She knew Jessie would disagree; after all, it was Jessie's job to deal with feelings. And for people who couldn't control their feelings, that was fair enough. But Alex could control her feelings. It had just been tricky lately because she'd been sick, and then sweet Lucy had died, and everything had gone crazy for a bit. But, day by day, her control was coming back. Last night she'd had an entire night without seeing Lucy's waxen hand reaching out to her. Not only that, but she wasn't spending all her time fighting back tears anymore. At last, she'd managed to push that emotional stuff back into the cupboard where it belonged. Soon, she planned to lock the door on it forever and throw away the key. Then she'd go back to the city.

Would she work for her father then? She had decided to leave that decision until later. Hopefully, Harley was right: she'd know when she needed to know. She smiled, imagining herself standing in front of the board of directors at Lockhart and Lockhart at one of their strategic planning meetings and saying: "Well, gentlemen, rest assured. We'll know when we need to know." What next? Beads and mocassins?

She wondered what it was going to be like to see Tom again. Tom. When she thought of him, she felt a surge of gratefulness. She knew he wasn't happy about her being here, yet he was doing everything he could to hold the fort at home. She hoped the visit here would help him to continue to do that, because there was no way she could go back yet. She needed more time.

If Jessie hadn't suggested it, the visit wouldn't be happening at all. And even so, Alex felt guilty about adding anything to Jessie's stress load. Lately, Jessie looked like she was at her breaking point.

But, Jessie had insisted, so Alex would try and keep her family out of everyone's way if she could.

As she thought about her family being here, she worried about Evan the least. He was going to fall in love with Luke and Sushi the minute he saw them, of that she was certain. Christina, however, would be another matter. "What will I do up there?" Christina had moaned when they'd talked about the visit, and Alex had wondered the same thing. There wasn't a movie theatre or mall at the end of the street. And Tom? How was Tom going to like it here? What would he think of Jessie and Harley? Bay Street comes to the Back Woods. It was going to be interesting.

It was strange how close she felt to Harley and Jessie now. There was no game-playing with people like that. Elfy was a no-nonsense kind of person as well. She just wished they'd give up this silly Save Wildwood business. The three of them didn't seem to understand the powers they were up against. Price had serious money, she could smell it. No one had a chance when serious money was involved.

And what was this thing Harley was suggesting, this sweat lodge? Jessie had tried to explain it to her, but how could someone's sweaty prayers to a bunch of dead ancestors be of any use? Was that the best he could come up with? No wonder native people had lost everything.

• • •

It starts when you're always afraid. The words sang out from the radio. Not wanting to hear them, she snapped the music off. Unfortunately, she couldn't turn off the truth of them. From the time she woke up in the morning until when she went to sleep, she could feel her fears running like mice along the nerve tunnels of her body. She was frightened about losing her home, frightened about what was going to happen to Sushi and the bird refuge, but most of all, she was frightened about the survival of the wilderness. If Price did what he wanted to do, the damage to the wilderness would be irreparable.

As she walked back out to the pool, she looked at the lush landscape around her. Unless she and The Grannies did something and did it soon, every tree, shrub and flower in front of her now would be obliterated, levelled for a fairway. A fairway that would be assaulted with hundreds of pounds of pesticides every year to keep it green, pesticides so poisonous that some toxicologists suggested golfers wash their hands after every game! Didn't the public realize these same pesticides ran off the golf course into the lake, contaminating every fish, turtle and duck that swam? What kind of denial prevented people from connecting the dots? It was as if some giant monster had crept up behind the human race and was muzzling its eyes and ears.

While Sushi swam around, she sat on the side of the pool. On a hot sunny day, the water was bright blue, reflecting the optimism of the sky, but today, because of the low, grey clouds, it looked lifeless and dull. She closed her eyes, wondering if she might sleep.

It was a funny thing about sleep deprivation. It blurred the distinction between what was real and what was unreal. Although she hadn't encountered it much during her years as a therapist, she had done some reading about it and knew that when a person was sleep-deprived, the need for dream time became so intense the person began to "dream" even when they were awake. These dreams, or hallucinations, could be so real, they were hard to distinguish from reality.

Was that what had been happening to her? A few times now, she'd thought something was happening when it hadn't happened at all. Yesterday, she'd been eating a banana, chewing it and swallowing it, when she'd realized there was no banana: her mind had dreamed it up. Her mind was dreaming up other things too, and sometimes it was hard to tell what was real. It was crazy-making. She'd visited people in mental institutions with a better grip on reality.

Harley was so concerned about her that, even though he had an early morning meeting at the rez about the casino, he'd done the night shift with Sushi. Even without the loon, she hadn't been able to sleep. She'd lain awake most of the night trying not to think about what she was trying not to think about. But, trying not to think about something was like trying *not* to see blue.

From her own experience as well as her work with clients, she knew thoughts were powerful. They were like mini-magicians, able to conjure up moods and incite all kinds of actions. That was why she was trying not to have the thought she kept having. She hoped that by not giving it a morsel of attention, it would shrivel up and die. But this thought, the thought she was trying *not* to have, had a life of its own. Not only had DJ invaded the lake, he had invaded her mind and she had to keep battling her thoughts every moment.

The problem was, battling took energy. And, with no sleep to rejuvenate her, she had no energy. Yet life kept pelting her with situations that needed her attention, so she stretched her resources to meet them, but it was like trying to stretch one sweater over too many cold bodies.

She'd worked with enough clients to know how close

she was to coming apart. She needed to be careful and not think about what she wasn't supposed to think about. In order to distract herself, she went to the car to get the envelope of Sushi's fan mail that Martha had given her a few days ago and brought it back to the pool. When she opened it, letters fell out. Some letters were appreciation for the work of the refuge, some asked questions, others asked about visiting. She'd have to write and tell the ones who wanted to visit that this wasn't possible. It was too stressful on the birds to have hordes of people gawking at them.

She looked at Sushi. "First you need your own personal minnow catcher, and now you need a secretary!"

When she opened the next envelope, a cheque fell out. She waved it happily in the air. "A donation to the minnow fund!" In last week's column, Martha had reported that Sushi was now sloshing down several dozen minnows a day and she'd made a special appeal for donations. Obviously, her appeal had worked.

Finally, something good was happening. When Harley returned from the rez, he would be pleased about this. She read the rest of the letters and was laying them aside when familiar arms came around her and pushed her into the pool.

"Oh, Harley," she said, coming up for air.

This was another of their games, sneaking up on each other. Except every time she tried to suprise him, he was ready for her. He seemed to have a radar about her and where she was.

Standing in front of her now, in T-shirt and cut-off jeans, his black hair glistened with water. Pulling her to him, he lifted her up so that her legs wrapped around his waist.

"Is this the opposite of a piggy back? A piggy front?"
He replied by kissing her. "You okay? You look beat."
She shrugged. "I'm getting used to it. How was it at
the rez? They going to go for the casino?"

"Headed that way," he said.

"It's ludicrous! Like nuns running a brothel to raise
money for a church!"

He spun her around in the water. "Let's sell this place.
Head north. Or out west. Build a cabin in the woods.
Deep in the woods."

Jessie groaned. "Wouldn't that be just running away?"

Harley looked at her quietly, then tossed the troll to
the far side of the pool. Sushi zoomed through the water
just under the surface, grabbed it in his beak and brought
it back. As Harley reached for it, Sushi darted away.

Jessie watched them play. To Harley, Sushi was a
brother. A *relation!* Part of his emotional-spiritual "body"
in the same way a hand or foot was part of his physical
body. To Harley, there was no separation between himself
and the animals or the rivers or the trees. They were all
living cells in the same organism. She understood now
why the natives had laughed when they first heard white
men say they wanted to "buy" the land. It was like saying
you wanted to buy someone's hand or a foot!

Harley fed Sushi several minnows, but the loon
pecked for more.

"Oink, oink," Harley said.

"So much for the expression 'eat like a bird'," Jessie
said. Then she remembered about the cheque. "Oh, look,
Sushi's fans have come to the rescue." She showed Harley
the letter.

He smiled and they watched Sushi spread the oil from

the duct near his tail over his feathers with his beak. Preening was what kept him waterproof. If water ever got in under his feathers, he would sink like a ball of clay.

Harley lay down in the pool and floated on his back. Jessie watched as the clear water slid over his smooth skin, and his long hair spread out on the water like a fan. Lazily he reached up and stroked Jessie's thighs.

"Elfy's due to arrive any minute," she told him.

"Make her day," he said, not stopping.

"Her month," she said. "Maybe even her year. But Luke will be running up the steps any minute, too. He's off catching minnows in the lake." She looked into Harley's eyes. They were as black and gentle as the night, and full of the fireflies of pleasure. Harley was the kind of man who got pleasure from giving it. And he certainly knew how to do that. It was as if he could feel what she was feeling. He slipped his fingers under the gusset of her bathing suit. Seeing Alex come out of the woods, Jessie eased away.

Harley tilted his head back and howled into the sky.

Jessie squeezed his hand. "You're crazy…"

"I never pretended to be sane…"

"Take a lot of pretending…"

They watched Alex go inside.

"I wish she'd cry," Jessie said. She couldn't see how Alex was going to move forward if she kept the brakes on her emotions like this. When someone distrusted their feelings as much as Alex did, the healing process took so much longer.

"I wish *you'd* cry," Harley said.

"I don't think crying will be easy for a woman like Alex," Jessie said, side-steping his comment.

"Her tears are close…" Harley said.

"She's definitely softening up," Jessie said. At least the woman no longer held her shoulders up to her ears. "I actually saw her laugh the other day." Alex hadn't made any sound when she laughed, but she might one day, Jessie thought, when her chest loosened up. But that was only going to happen if she let go of those tears. And if she did, it was going to be a gusher.

Harley looked at her with quiet concern. "When was the last time you laughed?"

Jessie winced. "There hasn't been much to laugh about," she said, hearing the defensiveness in her voice. She did not want this conversation.

Not now. "Anyway, is it all right with you if Alex stays for a bit?"

Harley shrugged. "Things arrive. Alex. Price. The casino. They bring teaching."

Jessie nodded. There he was, accepting what came his way again. Moving aside to make room for something else.

"But, aren't there some things a person should not make room for? Some things you simply have to fight, because they're right to fight?" She watched him consider this.

"Maybe. But if it's right for you to fight, that's because it's right inside you, not because of anything outside yourself. That's where people get screwed up. They think what's right for them to do is what's right for everyone." He looked at her pointedly.

"That's the big question, isn't it? Knowing what's right. Inside."

"And you can't figure that out until you know what your life is about, what your life is trying to teach you."

"But how can a person know if someone else isn't just running away? Because it's easier."

Harley was quiet. "You can't know the teaching of another. It's too tied up to their relationship with Spirit." His eyes held hers. He stretched his arms to the sides and swished the water in two places with his fingers. A troop of ripples rode toward each other. Watching the rings, she noticed that each ring handled the water coming at it in its own unique way. This made her think about clients.

"Horrible day," one client might say, coming in the door on a rainy day.

"It's magical," another would offer.

Same weather—two different attitudes. What a person said about the weather was more revealing than an ink blot test, Jessie thought. It made her think of that quote by Anaïs Nin: "We don't see things as they are, we see things as we are."

It was incredible the way people gave their power away. As if the weather, a lover, a boss, traffic, could "make" a person feel anything. Feelings were feelings. People or situations merely brought them out. She sighed. It all came down to blame, really. If we imagine someone can make us feel something, then it's easier to blame them for what we feel. Blame was such a hiding place. A seductive hiding place at that.

Lately she'd heard that even colours and sounds didn't exist in the world, but were created by the brain. Was there any such thing as an external reality? Maybe what was out there was simply a house of mirrors? A bumblebee buzzed through the air above the pool, and she thought for a moment about the world that an insect with compound eyes would see. Obviously, what someone called objective reality wasn't "objective" at all, but simply a group of agreed-upon details!

Just as she was thinking this, DJ's jet-ski roared out into the bay and headed full speed towards Bird Island. Screeching and cawing, the alarmed birds took to the sky, flying back and forth like a hundred handkerchiefs waving for help.

"And so it starts," Harley said.

Jessie grimaced. Most days DJ spent four to five hours out there. She had tried to talk to him, neighbours had tried to talk to him, but nothing had worked. They had tried reason, and the boy had rejected reason. Like a spoiled child, he was pushing the limits, then pushing the limits some more. And he'd keep pushing, she thought, until someone gave him a limit and held him to it. Someone was going to have to bite the bullet and take action. Which brought her back to the thought she was trying so hard not to think. Since she had the perfect way to stop him, in fact the only way that had even a slight possibility of working, wasn't it her responsibility to do it? She turned so she was face to face with Harley.

"I've been having this thought," she said. "Actually, I've been trying not to have it. But it seems to have me." She looked away. It was hard to talk about this and look at him.

He became still, apprehensive. He waited until her eyes came back to him.

She couldn't say it directly. "The thought is that someone should do something."

His eyes darted out to DJ's boat, then came back to her. He didn't miss her meaning. "Someone?"

She wanted to look away, but his eyes wouldn't let her. "Would that be such a bad thing?"

He sucked his top lip into his mouth and shrugged. She could tell from his eyes that for him, this wasn't a matter of bad or good. His face looked sad and full of pain.

"Think consequences," he said softly.

He put his arms gently around her, brought her in close and rocked her from side to side. "And think about that cabin we could build. Far away in the woods." When he spoke again, his voice was full of lament.

"Jail's not my favourite place," he whispered. "To stay or visit."

Chapter 11

Alex heard a car pull up and pricked her ears. Being a city person, she was used to crazies and cranks, so she wasn't as on edge as everyone else in the house, but she, too, felt uneasy. As The Grannies lit the fire under the Save Wildwood campaign, the entire community began to heat up. There were letters to the editor in every issue of the paper, as well as articles discussing the pros and cons of the development, but it was the pranks that took things to the boiling point.

First, Jessie had found the dead mice guts in her car. Then, a few days later, someone had tarred and feathered Wildwood's docks. After that, there had been threats to Sushi. It was the threats that had Jessie and Harley frantic. Harley took the threats seriously and spent most of one day wrapping wire netting around the pool to protect the loon, but as he said, someone with a 22-gauge shotgun would have no difficulty picking Sushi off.

Alex thought they were overreacting, but noticed herself listening and watching anyway. When she heard car doors slam, she relaxed. People who made that much noise were probably not people she had to be concerned about. She returned to reading her newspaper, and soon enough she heard the car driving away again. In a few moments, however, Jessie called to her. The urgency in Jessie's voice made Alex hurry up the stairs towards the loud peeps and cheeps on the main floor. Reluctantly, she went into the bird room and found Jessie hunched over a basket. Alex peeked in and saw a clump of tiny beaks and wrinkled skin. Beside her, Elfy was tending to a larger bird.

"I can see the cat's claw marks for crying out loud," Elfy said.

Alex tensed. She did not want to be involved in this. Jessie put a syringe of food into her hand.

"If we don't get some food into them fast, they'll die," Jessie said.

Dutifully, Alex copied Jessie, ejecting the food into the open mouth of one of the babies. The featherless bodies of the birds were so tiny that their heads looked huge. Some seemed to be having difficulty holding their heads up at all. Alex was doing her best to feed the smallest one when the bird collapsed, its body falling grotesquely over the others.

Jessie picked up the limp carcass and placed it on some towelling.

"One down," Elfy said.

Alex bit her lip and carried on. She did not look at the dead bird.

"We'll be lucky if any of these live," Jessie said.

Alex forced her thoughts back to the bird she was feeding. She wiped her brow. Why was it so warm in here? Feeling woozy, she forced herself to sit up straight, then held the head of the next bird in one hand while she injected food into its mouth with the other. The bird collapsed in her hand.

"Shit!" Alex tried again.

Beside her, Jessie's voice was soft. "You can't *make* it live."

Alex's throat hurt. She wanted to shout at Jessie but pressed her teeth together and carried on. Lucy's face appeared before her and something hot and sour rose up from her stomach. Pressing another plunger of the food-filled syringe into the next bird, she saw, with great relief, that it swallowed.

"Come on! Eat!"

The bird flopped over, its mouth full of food. Alex couldn't touch it, and again, Jessie lifted the bird's inert body out of the basket.

Alex worked faster now. She heard someone come into the room, but didn't look around. Smelling woods, she knew it was Harley. Then, as if to confirm it, she felt his hand move to her shoulder. She imagined turning and burying her head in his full chest. Snap out of it, she told herself, and made herself concentrate.

When the fourth baby died, Harley picked up the corpse with such gentleness that Alex felt her throat thicken, become spongy like a watermelon. Tenderly, he took Alex's hand, opened it and placed the dead bird in her palm. She turned her head away, refusing to look, but couldn't help but feel the waning warmth of its body on her skin. Her hand stiffened. She desperately wanted to drop the bird.

"Sad," Harley said.

One word. One softly spoken word. A fist of anguish shot up through her chest and throat, then collapsed back and tears burst out of her. Tears for Lucy, tears for her children, tears for all the sadness she'd never been able to express. Harley's large arms came around her and clutching the bird in her hand, she cried like a three-year-old.

• • •

Pellets of irritation exploded in Jessie's stomach. She checked her watch. She'd been waiting now for over an hour. *It's only an hour,* she told herself. *Calm down!* It worried her how hugely irritated she was getting by small things lately. It wasn't a good sign. If she ever got in to see the doctor, maybe she'd talk to him about this too.

She hadn't slept again last night and was so exhausted this morning, she decided to come here, to the medical clinic, before handing out flyers with The Grannies. Her plan was to ask the doctor for some sleep medication, but if she got up her nerve, she was going to ask for a prescription of Prozac. She needed to calm her mind down. If she didn't stop thinking about what she had to stop thinking about she was going to go crazy.

The clinic was crowded. After flipping through several magazines, she stood up and began to walk around. Then, before she knew it, her frustration pushed her out the door and into her car. She'd go to the doctor's another time.

"'Bout time you showed up," Elfy called as Jessie approached the liquor store where she was standing, flyers and a petition in hand. The flyer was bright yellow and had the words, "Save Wildwood" in bright red at the top. Below where the details of the upcoming community meeting.

Elfy looked at her with concern. "You look whipped."

"I feel whipped," Jessie said.

Elfy's eyes were full of compassion. "Still not sleeping?"

Jessie shook her head. "It's making me crazy."

"I can see," Elfy said. A man came out of the store and Elfy offered him a flyer. He ignored her. "One thing's sure. People are more interested in booze than birds." She looked down at her clipboard. "But I did get a few dozen people to sign the petition, so it hasn't been all bad. I wonder how the others are doing." Joey and Grace were around the corner handing out flyers in front of the A & P, and Estelle and Aggie were doing the same thing at Zeller's.

"Come on, let's take a break," Elfy said. "My feet are killing me."

They gathered up the others and headed for The Purple Pig. Soon, they were all settled at a round table in the corner, comparing notes.

"Hey, Jess," Joey said, "that's your fourth yawn. You all right? You don't look so good."

"Thanks," Jessie said, "thanks for the compliment."

Joey and Elfy exchanged glances. The waitress came, and they all gave their orders.

"Might as well give you one of these too," Elfy said, handing the waitress a flyer.

The waitress raised her eyebrow as she read it and wandered off.

"People sure give you the hairy eyeball when you do something like this," Joey said. "This morning some people were looking at me like I was wearing a sandwich board with something on it about the CIA." She laughed loudly, and a man at another table turned and looked at them.

"I have a colander you could borrow," Estelle said. "You could put that on your head. Just to complete the picture."

Joey didn't laugh. "The thing is, if we were eighteen and doing this, no one would bat an eyelash."

"Yeah, people are used to kids kicking up a fuss," Elfy said. "Not itty-bitty old ladies."

"Who're you calling itty bitty?" Joey said. The waitress deposited a plate of french fries in front of her. She picked one up, blew on it and shot it into her mouth.

"At our age, we're supposed to be knitting booties, not kicking ass!" Elfy said. She shook the mustard container and raised the lid of her hamburger.

Jessie sipped her tea. Tea was all she felt she could manage. "We're crazy old ladies now."

"I always wanted to be a crazy old lady." Elfy took a bite of her hamburger.

Aggie looked amused. "Elfy, you were born a crazy old lady."

Joey eyed Elfy. "The question is whether she's also The Loon?"

Elfy smiled. "If you want to know who The Loon is, head over to Jessie's."

Jessie groaned. She knew they were just fooling around but felt irritated anyway.

"That's where The Loon hangs out. In the pool there." Elfy's eyes glinted.

As Joey laughed, ketchup dripped off her french fry and landed on the table. Aggie pulled a thick wad of paper napkins from the dispenser.

Before she knew it, Jessie had reached out and blocked Aggie's hand. "Hey, not so many."

Jessie had meant to merely pause Aggie's motion, to give her a chance to consider whether she wanted to take so many napkins, but in her tiredness, she'd misjudged and used greater force than necessary. Aggie's arm bumped into Joey's arm and the french fry went flying.

"Jessie! What's the matter with you?" Aggie looked at her with hard eyes.

"Sure got quiet all of a sudden," Elfy said.

"Sorry, Aggie," Jessie said softly. "I didn't mean to be so rough. It's just that paper products are trees!" Everyone knew how she felt about trees.

"Yes, but you don't have to get crazy about it," Aggie said.

Elfy came to her rescue. "Since when is it crazy to try and save trees?"

Seeing the look of concern on everyone's faces, Jessie tried to explain. "It's just that if we're going to save the environment, that doesn't just happen out there. We have to take on what we do in our own lives too."

Elfy nodded. "It's a sham otherwise."

Joey frowned. "Yeah, but you have to live in the world! What are we supposed to do, stop driving? Stop using electricity? The way things are set up, if you're going to use resources at all, you can't not misuse them." She picked up one of the paper napkins and cleaned up the ketchup. "Even if I just used one of these, it still comes from a tree."

Jessie pushed the other napkins back into the dispenser. She wished she could go home and pull the covers over her head.

"All the more reason to use just one!" Elfy took a bite or her burger.

Aggie put down her grilled cheese sandwich and patted her mouth with an embroidered napkin she took from her purse. She narrowed her eyes at Elfy. "That hamburger's no better."

Elfy pushed the food to the side of her mouth and rolled her eyes. "Why do I feel the onset of a Sermon on the Mount?"

"There was an article about it in Time," Aggie said. "How Third World countries are cutting down *hundreds* of acres of rainforest every day so they can raise the beef, and *you* can eat a hamburger."

Although Jessie was hardly going to throw this into the fray, she'd received an e-mail that day saying that Brazil was planning to cut the Amazon Rainforest by fifty percent.

Elfy put the burger down. "I'm glad to hear you're getting so ecological, Ags. Does that mean you're going to change to cloth diapers instead of using Depends?"

"Ouch!" Estelle said, wincing.

Joey looked at them all with disgust. "Price would be grinning from ear to ear if he heard us squabbling like this."

They were all silent for a few minutes. No one was eating now, and the waitress came and cleared the table.

"How did it go at the tribunal?" Grace asked Jessie in a quiet voice.

Yesterday, she and Alex had gone to the Landlord and Tenant tribunal in a last ditch effort to see if they could fight the eviction through legal means. "It was just as Alex predicted," she said. "We don't have a legal leg to stand on."

"We all knew that," Aggie said.

"Still," Estelle said, "it's depressing."

"That means the community meeting is going to be all important," Aggie said, trying to rouse the waning spirits. She turned to Jessie. "Can I ask how the speech is going?"

"Fine," Jessie said. In truth she hadn't started it. When

did she have time to write a speech?

Joey grinned. "Make it a knock 'em dead one like you did for the tree campaign."

"No pressure there," Jessie said suppressing a yawn.

"Okay," Joey said, pulling out a pad. "Jess is doing the speech, Aggie, the slide show about the history of Wildwood, and Elfy, you're going to give all the stats about the bird refuge."

"I heard Price has hired a tree demolition company," Estelle said in a funereal voice.

Elfy pounced. "Who told you that?"

"Price told his receptionist," Estelle said, "who told my hair dresser, who told me."

Joey stopped sucking on her straw.

Elfy's face was dark. "That's bad."

Around her, everyone nodded. For the first time today, they were in complete agreement.

• • •

When Christina, Luke and Tom arrived, they sat awkwardly on the deck of the guest quarters. Alex felt tense.

"Would anyone like lemonade?" Alex asked. Tom and Luke shook their heads, but Christina cast a sullen look at the overcast sky and shivered. Rain had been threatening all morning. When she'd invited them, she'd imagined they would spend all their time outside in the sun and water, not crammed into the little apartment.

"If I'd made hot chocolate, it would have been warmer," Alex said. No one laughed. "It's an old camping joke, you know: if you remember the suntan lotion, it's sure to rain."

"Oh, yeah," Evan said.

Alex crossed her arms. "Speaking of hot chocolate, would anyone like some?"

"Me!" Evan said.

Christina examined her nails. "Whatever."

There was a slapping noise, and they all looked up.

"What the f—frig, is *that?*" Christina asked.

"It's cool," Luke said, approaching with a large black bird on his tanned arm. He was in his bare feet and wearing a pair of cut-off shorts, despite the cool weather.

Evan's eyes grew large as he edged closer. "What is it? A crow?"

"Raven," Luke said. "Part of his wing's gone. That's why he's not flying." The large bird moved up Luke's arm, then hopped on his head. "He wants to be a hat." He laughed.

Christina's eyes softened, then she looked away. Alex introduced everyone.

"How many birds do you have in the refuge?" Tom asked.

"Anywhere from two to two dozen," Luke said. "We don't usually let people look at them, it freaks them out—but if you use the binoculars, you guys can."

"Mom says there's a baby loon." Evan said.

"Sushi. Wanna see him?"

Evan trotted after Luke while the raven tried to keep his place on Luke's shoulder.

Tom stood up and went to the railing, his hands in his pockets. He rocked back and forth on his feet. The change in his pocket jingled. "It's like Camp Ahmanee, don't you think, Al?"

"Can I watch a movie, Dad?" Christina asked, her voice bored.

"You bring some? Sure."

Alex flinched. "There's no TV.

Christina crossed her arms and closed her eyes. Alex went into the cottage, ostensibly to make some coffee, but really to gather her resources. She didn't feel ready for this. Her throat felt sore again. When she came back out, she was relieved to see Harley and Jessie had come to say hello.

"We're going up to Floater's Bay," Jessie told them. "For a picnic. Want to come?"

"A picnic?" Christina looked at Alex with disdain.

Harley looked at Christina with amusement. "They call it Floater's Bay 'cause they found a body floating there once." When Christina looked up at him, he said, "Story is, a girl drowned her mother there."

Christina smiled, unsure whether to believe him, then looked away.

Alex and Jessie went inside to make sandwiches, and Harley wandered off to borrow the neighbour's aluminum boat. When they were ready to go, the boys scrambled up to the bow and the rest of them waved to Elfy, who was staying to look after Sushi. By the time they got to Floater's Bay, the sun was coming out.

Alex couldn't remember the last time she'd been swimming. At first she did the breaststroke, trying not to get her hair wet, but Evan splashed her until she dove, and she swam for as long as her breath would carry her. It was lovely to feel the coolness of the water on her body. She had forgotten the delight of this. She surfaced further down the shore and stood, looking back at everybody. Jessie, Harley and the boys were playing frisbee, yelping as they jumped and lunged. When Luke next had the frisbee, he tossed an easy pitch to Christina, who was still in the boat. She threw it back listlessly.

"Good one!" Luke shouted.

The others began throwing to Christina, and soon she was in the water too. Alex smiled, and looking around for Tom, saw that he had swum way out. His arm shot up and waved, and she waved back, then waved at her kids. This was something else she had forgotten: how wonderful it was to have her family near. Tears came to her eyes, and she didn't wipe them away.

Then a plane went by overhead, and she waved at it too. She'd seen this plane before, either landing or taking off, and she wondered to whom it belonged. The plane made her think about her mother. Would her mother ever get in a plane again? Alex couldn't even remember the last time her mother had been out of the house.

Funny, Alex thought. She had always thought it was her father she was closest to, but it had been her mother who had pried Alex's telephone number out of Tom, her mother who phoned every few days, her mother who asked if she could do anything to help. The other day, she'd even offered money if Alex needed it. Alex was surprised. She was aware of her mother's ample financial resources, but as far as she knew, they were locked up in the vault of her father's control. Was this not so? Maybe there was more to Shirley Lockhart than she let on.

After swimming, Harley, Tom and the kids gathered sticks from the woods, and Harley made a bonfire.

"Let's go get some fish," Harley said and headed towards the boat. The boys followed, and Harley waved to Christine, who rolled her eyes, but went along too.

Tom collected more wood and Alex and Jessie wrapped potatoes and put them in the coals. When Tom came back, he opened a beer and sat with them near the fire.

"Ever heard of Camp Ahmanee?" he asked Jessie.

"It's The Ahmanee Golf and Country Club now," Jessie said. "Building golf courses is the new Muskoka pastime."

Tom put his palms together and tapped his fingers against his mouth quietly.

Jessie looked into the fire. "People come up here for the wild beauty. The question is, will there be any of it left?"

Tom sipped his beer. "One of my clients is Eco-Golf. Heard of them?"

Jessie shook her head.

"They're developing what they call 'ecological golf courses'."

Jessie grimaced. "Still means taking down hundreds of trees."

"Yes, but it means leaving hundreds as well." He smiled at her affably.

Alex nodded. "Shopping malls don't spare any." The longer she stayed here, the more she found herself resisting Price's development idea. But he owned the land, so what could anyone do?

Tom continued. "Properly set up, golf courses can be wonderful nature reserves."

"I just wish my house wasn't on the chopping block," Jessie said.

Tom looked at Alex with alarm, and seeing her nod, brought his eyes back to Jessie. "Where are you going to live?"

Alex could see the tension pulling at Jessie's face. Lately she looked like someone suffering from a continual headache. Alex was worried about her. How could anyone do all that Jessie was doing: see clients, run a bird refuge, fight to save Wildwood? It was too much, way too much.

Jessie looked at Tom. "Where am I going to live? The way things are going, it might just be the loony bin!"

Alex frowned. It scared her to hear Jessie talking this way. The woman was on the edge, there was no question about it.

Hearing a boat, Alex turned and saw Harley coming back with the kids. Evan held a fish up like a prize.

While Harley gutted their catch, the boys went for another swim, then they all ate fish and potatoes and roasted marshmallows. On the way home Alex watched Evan. Harley was letting him drive the boat, and she'd never seen her son look happier. Beside her, Luke was showing Christina various knots and although her daughter wasn't exactly grinning, she didn't appear as grumpy as she had earlier.

Closer to home, a jet-ski was zooming up and down the lake.

"Whoa," Evan said, "that boat's going FAST."

"The speed of death itself," Alex heard Harley say. She watched Jessie's eyes track the boat up the lake.

When it had disappeared, Alex faced the front again. She wanted to feel the cooling wind on her face. She couldn't remember the last time she'd had so much sun. It made her think of her days at camp. How incredibly carefree she'd been. What she would give for some of that feeling now.

"What's that?" Christina said, pointing.

Harley saw it at the same time and put his hand over Evan's on the throttle, slowing the boat down. Something black was thrashing about in the water, a few hundred yards away. Taking over the steering, Harley steered over to it, then cut the motor.

The bird was flipping every which way, obviously in great distress. Because of its agitation, it was difficult to see what kind it was.

Jessie looked at Harley. "A loon?"

Harley's face was stricken. "*Was* a loon."

Then she saw what Harley had already seen, and she understood why the loon had been struggling: one of its legs was broken in half like a toothpick.

Harley dug the paddle into the water and brought the boat to where the bird was flopping around. Leaning forward, he scooped the baby from the lake. As he passed the bird to Jessie, it burst from his hands and landed in Alex's lap. Alex was startled but knew enough to hold on to it and not let it go.

Up close, they could see the loon's leg bone sticking out through the skin.

"What happened—" Evan whispered, "what happened to its foot?"

Harley did not answer, only looked up the lake to where the jet-ski had gone.

Alex couldn't take her eyes off the poor bird. "Will it live?"

"If it does, it will regret it," Harley said.

Jessie beat her fists into the air. "That fucking bastard! That fucking, fucking bastard!"

Alex, like everyone else, stared at her in silence.

Jessie collapsed and thrust her head down into her hands. When Luke reached out to touch her shoulder, she pushed him away.

Chapter 12

Dressed in a midnight-blue jacket, Jessie paddled quietly into the dark lake. It was sometime in the middle of the night and everything was so black, she could barely see the buoy. There wasn't even a sliver of a moon. The less light the better, she thought. And the lake was calm, dead calm. That was a good sign too. All of nature seemed to be on her side.

The rope was coiled at her feet, ready. She'd wondered about blackening it so it wouldn't be visible, but if things went according to plan, it would be under water anyway. To make sure it sank, she'd tied sinkers to it every foot or so. That would weigh it down.

Every time she thought about the fractured leg of the new loon, her fury whipped itself into a frenzy again. When they had taken it to the animal clinic, she'd hoped the vet would be able to save the leg, or at least the foot, but the bone had been too badly damaged. The vet had left as much of the leg as he could to help the bird with balance, but he'd been forced to amputate the foot. As yet, she couldn't look at the stick of leg without wanting to vomit.

The loon himself was showing incredible courage. They had him home now and swimming and he was impressing everyone with his gumption. So they gave him that name: Gumption.

When they brought him home, they'd all been concerned about the two loons getting along. Sushi, however, established himself as top bird right from the start, and Gumption seemed content with his position, so there had been no problems. The only challenge was the extra work. But Evan was staying on for a visit and like Luke, he adored the loons, so they had lots of help. And Christine had called several times to find out how Gumption was doing. Even Alex was doing some loon sitting from time to time.

Jessie felt bad that most of the work with the loons fell to the boys. It worried her every time they were out in the pool unsupervised. What if someone took a shot at one of the loons and missed? *Stop it!* Thoughts like this just cranked her up, and what had happened to Gumption had her cranked up enough already. It was such a tragedy. A tragedy DJ was responsible for. There was no doubt in her mind now. The kid was a menace and had to be stopped. That's why she was out here now.

When she was beside the buoy, she tied the rope to the metal wire that fixed the drum to the cement block at the bottom of the lake. The water slipped over her hands, silky and alive. It felt like a greeting. She imagined the water knew her mission and was wishing her well, as she imagined most of the people on the lake would do if they knew what she was doing. Everyone wanted DJ stopped. It was just that she was the only one who knew how to do it.

As she paddled back, she turned to see if the rope was sinking. To her great relief, she saw that it was. The fates were with her! She hoped that the fates would continue to be with her and everyone would think the accident a stupid mistake. The kind of mistake a half-brained teenager like DJ was all too likely to make. Meanwhile, as his boat was out of commission, she and the wildlife on the lake would have weeks of quiet celebration.

Back at the shore, she pulled up the canoe and secured the other end of the rope to a tree. Now, the trap was set. Ready for DJ day. All she had to do was wait for his boat and pull. Would she do it? *Could she do it?* If DJ had come out on his jet-ski right this very moment, she would have, but then she was very angry. She'd have to see what she felt like when she calmed down. If she ever did calm down.

She looked up. The stars were like a thousand watching eyes. What would they think if she did this? Surely, such great natural forces as these would understand that universal laws and human laws were not always in agreement. And that human laws were still evolving. She couldn't imagine that this greater wisdom wouldn't support her efforts to reestablish the balance. In fact, wasn't it her responsibility to do so? If that meant acting like a kind of ecological Robin Hood, then she was willing to do that. Someone had to. All living things had the right to be honoured. Sometimes that meant standing up and sticking your neck out!

She thought of some of her heroes: Karen Silkwood for exposing the contamination at a nuclear plant, Dian Fossey for trying to stop the annihilation of mountain gorillas, Hilda Murrell, a seventy-eight-year-old woman in England, who had launched a strident opposition to nuclear waste. These were no ordinary women. They had all been willing to stand up for what they believed. The problem was, all these women had been murdered.

She walked back to the house, trying not to think about this, but her stomach churned anyway.

• • •

"Fire keeper? What's a fire keeper?" Alex asked. Evan was wiggling with excitement as he stood by her bed. She yawned. Dawn was just breaking and she wasn't awake yet.

"Harley's building the sweat lodge!" Evan said. "He says Luke and I can do the fire!"

"And that's all you'll be doing?" Alex asked.

Evan nodded. "Please?"

She looked at her son. Had he grown? Put on weight? There was something different about him. He seemed more substantial somehow. Reluctantly, she gave him the go-ahead. "But I'll be watching," she told him. With all the pranks and threats going on, she planned to keep a close eye on things. "Take your inhaler!"

When she got out of bed a while later, the inhaler was still sitting on top of the fridge. Had he even used it lately? She didn't think so. Up until a few weeks ago, he'd kept it on a string around his neck.

She made a cup of coffee and took it out to the deck. This sweat lodge thing made her nervous. Over the last while, she'd talked to Harley a lot about her father and her work and what to do. For some reason, Harley had the idea that doing this "sweat" would help her. Hoping he'd forget about it, she had said nothing, but now, here it was, being planned right in front of her.

In fact, she could see Harley and the boys in a clearing not far away. Alex waved to them and opened her newspaper. Although she hadn't intended to listen in, it was a still day and she could hear almost everything Harley was saying.

Harley began by telling the boys that "a sweat" as he called it, was a sacred ceremony that natives had been using for thousands of years as a way of aligning their souls with The Great Spirit. He lit a match and held it under a bundle of dried weeds.

Alex sniffed the air. Was that marijuana? As weird smelling as it was, she didn't think so. Were they going to smoke it? Peeking from behind her newspaper, she watched as Harley took what looked like the wing of a bird and swept the smoke from the herbs around himself. As he did this, he spoke some words in Ojibway. Wasn't that the language Jessie said he spoke?

Harley was sweeping the smoke around the boys now. What was this, some sort of purification ritual? She watched her son close his eyes. Evan was going to start coughing any moment now. Smoke always did that to him. And when he did, she'd have the perfect excuse to call him in and end this silliness. But, as the smoke swirled around him, Evan stood as still as a tree, his face serene. She had never seen him look this way before and felt a moment of panic. Being up here was bringing out a side of him she'd never seen. He was taking to this place like a duck to water. Last week, he'd asked if they could move up here. Silly goose.

She was interrupted by a phone call from Christina. Christina called often now, wanting to know about Gumption.

"I did a drawing of the loons for art class," Christina said. "It's awesome."

"Are they screaming?" In the last few years, every drawing her daughter did involved screaming.

"Mom!"

"Sorry." Alex told Christina what her brother was doing.

"Cool," Christina said, clipping the word like all kids did.

"No, hot! They're not going to catch me in there."

"Oh, mom, don't be so OLD."

Alex tried not to show her hurt and chatted about other things. When she got off the phone, she went back out on the deck.

Now Harley was telling the boys they were going into the forest to collect the heating stones, and that it was important to ask the stones if it was all right to move them.

Had Alex heard right?

"Ask who?" Evan asked.

Good question! Alex waited for Harley to speak. Was he going to tell them there were stone fairies? Nature gods? This was becoming more pagan by the minute. She sat up in her chair, more alert than ever.

Harley strode over to Evan, lifted him up and carried him a few feet away.

"Hey!" Evan yelled.

Harley put him down. "Sorry, should have asked."

"Okay, I get it." Evan grinned. "But I can talk. Stones can't."

"You sure?" Harley tapped his chest. "Try listening from here."

Over the next few hours, Alex watched as the three of them carried head-sized rock and armfuls of what looked like willow branches to the building site. By midafternoon, Harley and the boys had fashioned the saplings into a low, igloo-shaped structure and covered them with blankets and animal skins.

Alex regarded the structure and winced. It was so *small*. Small spaces made her nervous. From the huge pile of firewood they had gathered, she could see they were planning a big fire. That meant heat and lots of it. Between her fear of enclosed places and her dislike of hot ones, she wouldn't be able to stand it for more than five minutes. She'd just have to tell Harley that.

"I'm too OLD for this sort of thing," she imagined herself telling Harley. She winced. She didn't like the sound of that at all.

• • •

From deep in her sleeping bag, Jessie listened to the plick, plick, plick of the early morning rain on the canvas of the teepee. So this is what peace and quiet is like, she thought, smiling. Dear Harley. Ever since she'd talked to him about the thought she wasn't supposed to be thinking, he'd been so concerned about her that he'd had some men from the rez come and erect this teepee. They'd set it up in the woods, not too far from the house, but far enough to be a place where, as Harley said, "she could listen to herself."

What a different approach to healing, she thought. Most of her psychotherapeutic training encouraged people to solve their dilemmas by talking. And talking to someone else, a psychiatrist or psychotherapist who would help them sort it all through. Harley's way was to help a person get still enough that they could listen—to themselves, their ancestors, The Great Spirits. He believed that all things, both seen and unseen, were imbued with consciousness, therefore, one was never alone. But in order to "hear" the messages of these supporters, a person had to get very still.

She rolled over on her back. It felt comforting to lie with her body so close to the earth. Soothing. She and Harley had spent the night out here, and even though she still hadn't slept much, she felt more rested. That was the awful thing about sleep deprivation: not sleeping made her tired, and when she was tired, she wasn't able to ward off her worries, which then cranked her up until the possibility of sleep was even further away. It was an emotional merry-go-round.

But this morning, she felt a little less scared of all she had to face. As Harley kept reminding her, there were still wild places that would open their arms to them. He'd take off in a heartbeat, that she knew. But leaving still felt like running away. She couldn't, wouldn't allow herself to do that.

Was she going to do it? The other night, when she'd been out on the lake setting up the rope, it had felt like an imperative. It was as if the well-being of the lake, the birds, of all wild things demanded that she protect them. Of course, that had been right after finding Gumption and seeing his mutilated leg. It still infuriated her to think about him. Sushi's plight had been scary enough, but at least one day he'd be able to fly. Gumption would never be able to do that.

But, at least it looked like Gumption was going to survive. And now that the crisis was over and she was resting here in the quiet, far away from the sound of any jet-skis, she could think better. Make up her mind whether to do it or not.

The flap to the teepee opened and Harley came in with an armload of twigs under a sheaf of birch bark.

Raindrops glistened on his hair. He put the wood in a pile, then picked up his fire-making bow. As Jessie watched, he wrapped the small, thumb-thick friction stick in the bow's cord, then stood the stick on a flat piece of notched wood where he'd curled some tinder. In an easy, rhythmical motion, he sawed the bow back and forth until there was a burning smell and then, a thin finger of smoke. When the smoke increased, he lifted the clump of tinder and gently breathed into it. The smoke thickened, becoming as dense and white as a cotton ball. Harley blew into it strongly now, and it erupted into flame. She'd watched him make fire dozens of times, yet each time, it was as magical as if he'd pulled a rabbit out of a hat.

She watched as he continued to build the fire. It was lovely to focus only on this. So often her mind was juggling so many details that none of them got much attention, but when she pulled her awareness out of her thoughts and onto what was happening around her, it was like putting on those 3-D glasses in the movies when she was a kid.

The moment she began thinking, however, the scene before her dulled. So, she let go of her thoughts once again and fell back into the lush world of her senses. Then, after a while, she closed her eyes and let herself float in the silence. Harley was right, the silence was lovely. She felt as if she might be able to find herself in it.

She remembered a conference she'd once attended at a Jesuit retreat centre. Wandering around at lunch time, she discovered a guest book and leafed through it. One of the comments written there was: *In the silence, the thread of the world is kept from breaking.*

She thought about those monks and all the other

people who guarded the silence, who stoked it daily with their own contribution of quiet and was grateful. She looked at Harley as he sat in perfect stillness in front of the fire, his face wide and open. His friendship with the quiet was one of the things she appreciated most about him. With Harley, it was easy not to talk. Harley had never been big on the verbal anyway, believing that when people talked too much, the words were usually empty anyway, like cups drawn from a well that hadn't had time to fill.

Leaning forward, she kissed his mouth. She could feel her kiss go into him like a shiny coin dropping into clear water. He wrapped his arms around her and pulled her close and they sat staring at the fire. The office manager in her brain told her she should get up and attend to the dozens of details of the campaign or think about the needs of the birds, but luckily for her, Harley began touching her and the sensations in her body became louder than the voices in her head.

Afterwards, she stroked the round curve of his chest. "So, how long do you think I can hide out here?"

"Be nice and I'll make sure it's a while."

"Thought I was being nice."

"You could always be nice again."

She smiled and rolled over. Beside her she could feel Harley drifting into sleep. He had the ability to sleep anywhere at any time. Never had she known a man so at peace with himself. Was she at peace with herself? No. And she wouldn't be until she resolved this thing about DJ. Was she going to do it or not?

Her prime motive was to stop DJ from hurting the birds. He was endangering wildlife, and she felt a protective need to stop him, as she might stop anyone from hurting something she loved. When she thought like this, she felt justified in doing what she was contemplating. Yes, DJ's boat would be damaged, but she could deal with that. Even if she got caught for damaging it, she would be willing to take the consequences. There might be a fine. She might even be charged with a small misdemeanour, but she could handle that. She smiled wryly. What if they made her buy the boy a new boat? Wouldn't that just be the joke of the decade?

But there was more at stake here than DJ's boat. What if the boy himself got hurt? She knew it was unlikely; after all, even if he fell off the jet-ski, he was only going to land in the lake. But still, what if by some strange twist, he wrenched his back or twisted an ankle? Or worse? Could she live with herself?

If she got caught, there would be other repercussions too. Her career as a psychotherapist, for example, would be thrown into serious jeopardy. Even though she wasn't sure she wanted to do this type of work anymore, still, it was another thing to have it end in disgrace. And if she was disgraced, she wouldn't even be able to run a bird refuge. No one would trust her. She would become an outcast in her own community.

So, give it up, she told herself. It's not worth it. Yet something pushed her on. Fuck off. Fuck off! His words replayed in her mind as they had a thousand times. All she wanted was to get back at him. Was that what this was about? Retaliation? She definitely wanted to teach him a lesson.

Waking up, Harley rolled on his side towards her. She could feel the heat of his body radiating towards her.

"Do you think you can teach someone something?" she asked.

Harley rubbed his eyes. "Not unless they're ready to learn it." He looked at her seriously. "You're still thinking about it, aren't you?"

Jessie nodded.

He put his hand on her chest, and she could feel her heart beating against his fingers.

"What's this part of you say?"

She groaned. "I don't know."

She looked him fully in the eyes. "Think I should do it?"

He became very still. "Take it to the sweat."

Chapter 13

When Alex awoke from her nap, she smelled smoke. Startled, she sat up and saw the boys standing near a large fire several feet from the completed sweat lodge. Realizing they must be getting close to starting, she put on her bathing suit and headed for the far side of the house. She'd go for a long swim and make herself scarce. Then they'd get tired of waiting and start without her and that would be that.

"Hey!"

Alex turned. Elfy was sitting by the pool, babysitting the loons. She held up a letter.

"For me?" Alex said, staring at it as if it were a foreign object. She took it from Elfy and was about to say "thank you" when she saw her father's handwriting. She tried to swallow but couldn't. Waving dumbly at Elfy, she wandered over to the trees. Leaning against a trunk, she opened the envelope slowly, as if it might explode. The letter was written on company letterhead. Alex, it said at the top left. Not *Dear Alex*, just *Alex*. The sharpness of the words cut her.

"As of August 15th, your services to this company will no longer be required." At the bottom, it said, "Sincerely, Angus."

She let herself slide down the trunk of the tree until she was sitting on the ground. He had hired somebody else! Her worst fear had come true. An idea shot through her. Maybe if she drove down to the city, she could make him change his mind. She could leave now. Be there in two hours. Yes, that's what she should do, should have done weeks ago.

She stood up. At the periphery of her vision, something pulled at her attention. She looked up numbly and saw Evan waving. With effort, she raised her hand. Beside Luke, Harley and Jessie stood, dressed only in towels. Hadn't they started yet? What were they waiting for? She groaned, realizing to her great distress, they were waiting for her. Feeling utterly overwhelmed, she walked over to them. She must convince them to go ahead.

As soon as Harley saw her coming, he crouched down and entered the small opening into the skin-covered cave. Undaunted, Alex carried on. She'd explain to Jessie instead. But as Alex approached, Jessie went into the lodge too. Alex looked down at her bathing suit. No wonder they'd gone in, they thought she was coming to join them.

"But I—"

The boys stood at either side of the little door. Evan was grinning at her with pride and happiness. Dear Evan. He thought she was going to be a part of this too. She opened her mouth to tell them that she couldn't possibly do this, when the flap opened.

"Good luck, Mom," Evan said and suddenly kissed her.

She bent down and crawled in.

Inside the hut it wasn't hot at all. *I'll just stay a few minutes,* she told herself as she sat on a towel that had been spread over the hay-covered earth. Luke appeared at the door with a rock in the palm of his shovel. The rock had a reddish glow and she could feel its heat swell towards her as it was brought in and positioned in the fire pit in the centre of the lodge. Luke brought in three more rocks, then the flap was closed.

Alex thought she'd gone blind, it was so black. Then something glittered orange on the rocks and burnt hot and white like sparkling stars. The smell of pungent herbs filled the lodge. Then all was black again. She wiped her brow and realized she was still clutching the letter. It was sodden from the heat.

When Harley spoke, it was in Ojibway. His voice was deep and resonant and filled the cave. She could feel the vibration of it against her skin. Then, as the heat softened her, she felt the sound of it go right through her body.

"Oh, Great Spirit," he said, changing to English. "I call upon you and all our ancestors to help us at this time. I call on the four directions, the north, the south, the east and the west, that each may offer its wisdom to us tonight. I call upon the fire and the stones to purify us that we may hear the deep truth in our hearts."

More stones were brought in. The air became hotter, making it difficult to breathe. She shifted further back against the wall of the lodge, but there was no escaping the brutal sting of the heat. Sweat dripped down her body, soaking her towel. What was the point of this? She'd stay five more minutes, that was it.

Beside her Jessie whispered, "Breathe the heat into your belly. Let it in."

Let it in? She made an effort, and as she let go of her resistance, the heat wasn't so awful after that. She began to see faces in the stones. One of the faces looked like her father, but it was older than her father. It reminded her of her grandfather. Whoever it was seemed to be speaking to her, not in words, but in some other way and an understanding came into her about her father. At first she did not want this understanding. She was too angry at him, and feeling justified in her anger. He had hired someone else. How could he! But the heat softened the anger, and she could feel it dripping away, despite her wish to hold on to it. Then she began to realize how lonely her father was without her, and how little there was in his life now to make him happy. That was why he hadn't contacted her, because it was too painful for him. He missed her too much and was too angry at her for going her own way. Soon tears were streaming down her face along with the sweat. Now the grandfather stone seemed to smile at her.

The paper of her father's letter was hot, and her fingers tingled as she held it. Slowly she began folding it, first lengthwise, then bent each side at an angle, making a sharp nose like that of a paper airplane. She felt dizzy now and was glad to have the paper plane to focus on. When she'd been little, she'd made hundreds of paper planes. One of her favourite games had been to stand on top of a hill and, holding one of her planes high in the air, race down. Sometimes she imagined she was the plane zooming through the air and sometimes she imagined she was a bird. It didn't matter. What mattered was that she was flying.

Now, as she held the paper plane in her heat-frenzied state, something shifted in her brain, and she felt herself drop into a kind of waking dream. She heard a whooshing sound and felt a wing of wind sweep under her and lift her up and out of the sweat lodge. Then, suddenly, she was flying.

Whether she was dreaming or hallucinating, she didn't know or care. She was airborne. Like in her childhood dreams, she was gliding and sliding through the feathery air, swooping and soaring, free as a bird. Way down below, she could see her mother, smiling and waving up at her. She knew then, from her mother's face, that she didn't have to worry about her father. He was going to be fine. A feeling of freedom breezed through her. It was all right for her to fly. So, she spread her wings wider and flew further into the blue dream of sky.

• • •

As Jessie drove back from Rosie's, the woman who made homeopathic remedies for the birds, she took the back roads. It was her favourite time of day, early evening. In the height of summer, around eight o'clock, the sun had a way of lighting everything up, so the air looked bright and yellow, as if it were lit by a thousand invisible candles. The light was so strong and golden, she felt as if she could reach out and touch it. Just driving through it made her feel alive and full of hope.

Around her, the rolling fields were bursting with corn, potatoes, hay and barley. August was such a plump month, so willing to deliver the promises sown in spring. She smiled. She felt peaceful. All day she'd felt peaceful. It was as if the sweat had burned the confusion right out of her.

During the first part of the sweat, she hadn't thought much was happening. While Harley was speaking at the beginning of the ceremony, she'd focused on her breath and tried to create an open space for guidance to come to her. But guidance hadn't come. All that came was a weird image. She didn't like to think of it even now. What could it possibly mean? She shivered. His lips had felt so real against her own. And their mouths had been open so wide. Like those kisses in the movies. She had even pulled DJ's head towards her, to bring his mouth closer. But there had been no lust to the kiss. In fact, what she remembered was nausea. She cringed thinking about it.

When the flap had opened, signaling the end of the ceremony, she had felt a sinking disappointment. Then, as she searched around the hay floor for her water bottle, she'd felt something silky. In the dim light, she could just see it. It was a tiny, very white feather. She had almost cried out. To her, it was a message from the birds. It was a message telling her to focus on her work with them and leave this business about DJ behind.

With the feather held securely in her hand, she had crawled out of the skin igloo in search of Harley. She knew that to him, a synchronicity like this would be important. To him, it would be nature's way of answering her.

When she found Harley, he had looked strained and preoccupied.

"Are you all right?"

Harley shook his head. "I got a really bad feeling in there. Now I'm trying to figure it out." His black eyes found her. "I don't want you to—that thing with DJ, I don't want you—"

The boys were around them now, and it wasn't easy for them to talk. In an attempt to reassure him, she showed Harley the feather. "It's okay. Everything's okay."

Harley looked at her as if he was having a hard time believing this. Seeing that the boys wanted his attention, she kissed him on the forehead and went over to the outside shower to wash off. Then she went back to the teepee, thinking she'd see him there. But she was asleep when he came back and gone when she awoke in the morning. Had he slept outside? Whenever Harley needed solace, he sought the night. She wondered what he was so disturbed about.

After she woke up, she went to see if he was in his workshop, but he wasn't there either. While she waited for him, she gathered some leather and beads and made a necklace for the feather she had found in the sweat. If she was going to dedicate her life to birds, she was going to allow herself to wear feathers.

Now, as she drove through the golden evening, she reached up and touched the feather necklace. It felt silky in her fingers. Then, remembering that she'd promised Harley she'd pick up a part for the boat, she swung into the marina parking lot. Once upon a time, this marina had been a one dock operation. Now the place was like a small town, with parking lots, docks, forklifts to take boats in and out of the water and dozens of buildings to store the boats over the long winter months. People and kids and dogs moved in and around boats of every size, shape and colour.

As she made her way to the main building, she walked by the docks, where a boy with thighs the size of fire hydrants was gassing up a huge plastic boat with curved, sculpted seats and a darkly tinted windscreen. Looks like something from outer space, she thought. She hated it. The driver was wearing a neon pink shirt and mirrored sunglasses. The woman beside him had globular breasts. Probably plastic too, she thought, quickening her pace. All she wanted was to get her business done and get out of there.

Inside the main building, there were groceries, wet suits, skis and all kinds of boat accessories. As she stood in line, she looked out at the man with the mirrored glasses. When his boat was full of gas, he turned on the ignition and the engine roared to life. Then, leaving it running, he came inside.

Blips of irritation fired off inside Jessie's stomach. She hated it when people left their boats running like this. All that pollution going into the water just because someone couldn't be bothered turning a key.

"Hey, mister! You left your boat running!"

The man turned to her. In the mirrors of his glasses, she could see the face of an irate old woman. She tried to penetrate through the mirrors to his eyes, but couldn't. The man ignored her and moved away as if she hadn't spoken. Then, picking up some bags of potato chips, he tossed them on the counter. The boy began ringing up the sale.

"Thought I was next!"

Startled, the boy behind the counter looked up, viewing her with the same kind of caution one regards an animal with foam on its lips.

"Oh, go ahead," she said to the boy. There was no point in giving the kid a hard time because the man was being such an idiot. She wiped her forehead. Why was it so hot in here? And why was his boat so loud? The garbling sound was driving her nuts. She glared at him. *Get a move on!* She shook her head. Now he was trading his ketchup-flavoured potato chips for sour cream and onion.

"Take your time," she said.

The man with the potato chips finished paying for his things. Good, she thought. Now he'll drive his stupid boat away, but the man wandered over to the water ski equipment. The sales boy turned to her, but the sound of the idling motor was so loud in her ears, she couldn't concentrate.

"Just a minute!" She strode outside, jumped in the man's boat and turned the key.

"Hey!"

"Your boat pollutes enough as it is!"

He sneered and gave her the finger. His gesture was like a match to the dynamite of her mood. Sensing danger, she turned and ran to the car. She had to get out of here and she had to get out of here fast. Not bothering with her seat belt, she tore out of the parking lot. Her body felt like a cocked gun.

Speeding around the first corner from the marina, she hit the brake pedal hard. Just ahead, where the road cut through a swampy area, she saw a turtle. It was a real granddaddy, as big as a hubcap. She swerved violently, pleading with her car to miss it, pleading with the turtle to somehow get out of the way.

There was a thunking sound, and the car bounced up. She pulled over and got out of the car. The turtle's shell was cracked and beneath it there was a circular smear of blood. Its dead eyes looked right at her.

Slowly, very slowly, she got back into her car. Her joints felt stiff and old and it took a few moments to get the fists of her hands to unfurl so she could hold the steering wheel. A line of cars began to form behind her. Some of them honked, but she didn't care. The centre of her chest hurt. It was as if someone had punched her in the heart. She lifted her hand to touch her feather, but it was gone. Somehow, somewhere, it had slipped from her neck.

When she got back, she walked past the boys who

were out in the pool with the loons and went inside. She was relieved that no one was there. Her hands were shaking, but she went into the bird room and started washing cages. She felt an overwhelming need to clean. When she heard the jet-ski, the thought came into her mind again, but she had no energy to push it away.

As she walked through the woods, she knew she was going against what was true for her, what was right for her, but she was beyond that now. When she came to where she'd left the rope, she took it in her hands. The sound of DJ's boat was loud in her ears, louder than it had ever been. It was as if the sound of all the boats she'd ever heard was pressing into her ears, screaming into her brain.

Her fingers clamped the rope. She wouldn't have to pull the buoy far. Just far enough so it no longer marked the rocks. Then DJ would hit those rocks and the terrible noise would stop.

She closed her eyes. The rope felt soft as she held it, and she could feel it extending out, connecting her to a future she would be pulling towards her the moment she moved her hands. She shook out her fingers. They were cramping from gripping the rope so tightly. She lifted the rope in readiness—

BANG!

She looked up and saw DJ and the boat shoot into the air. The boat hurtled up and up, and then, when the violent force of its momentum could no longer sustain the weight, the boat paused at the height of the arc and the boy's body somersaulted over, then hit the water, just seconds before the boat crashed on top of him. Jessie's shoulders and head thumped down as if she herself had received the blow.

Chapter 14

Alex sucked the blood from her finger. She'd been biting her nails again. Usually she kept cool in a crisis, but this was a challenge. She moved the phone to the other ear and fingered the dry squares of crackers that sat beside the bowl of cold tinned soup. She really should eat.

When the receptionist answered, Alex put on her most professional voice.

"Mr. Hench, please," she said. "Tell him it's Alex Lockhart. It's important!"

Music erupted in her ear as she was put on hold. Although semi-retired now, Hench was one of the best criminal lawyers in Toronto. Luckily for Jessie, luckily for everyone, Alex had handled his investment portfolio for years and knew him well enough to ask a favour.

"Alex!" Hench said in his gruff, bull-dog voice. "How the hell are ya?"

Keeping her tone light, she told him the basics of what had happened.

"They'll lock her up and throw away the key, if she's guilty," Hench said when Alex had finished. "That's if the kid dies. The minute there's a body, people want blood."

Alex could hear the click of his lighter. Hench loved his cigars.

"What'd she say to the cops?"

"That she didn't do it."

"Good, but I hate to tell you, that's what they all say."

Alex was quiet. Part of her wanted to defend Jessie, but in truth, she didn't know what to think. Even if Jessie had done it, would she admit to it? Who in their right mind would confess to doing such an horrendous thing, specially when the consequences were so dire? But if Jessie didn't do it, why had she set it up like that?

"The kid going to live?"

Alex cleared her throat. This was the difficult part. "No one seems to know."

"Damn tricky things, comas," Hench said. "I had a client in one for two years once. Lay there like a cooked carrot."

Alex heard Hench puff on his cigar and asked, "Did your client live?"

"Hell no! Family had to pull the plug. Terrible to say, but dying is better than the never-never land of a coma. With a coma, the hell just goes on and on."

Alex cringed.

Hench lowered his voice. "Between you and me, Alex, she guilty?"

Alex heard the loud breath of her sigh go into the phone. It was all so confusing. "I don't think there's much doubt that she both planned it and set it up. The kid had been driving everyone crazy. There's probably not a person on the lake who didn't want him stopped. But I don't think she wanted to actually hurt him. Otherwise, she wouldn't have tried to save him."

"She tried to save him?"

"She went out and hauled him out of the water." Alex doubted if DJ would be alive if Jessie hadn't done what she'd done.

"Guilt can be a funny thing." Hench was quiet. "We'd

better get the forensic guys up there."

Alex nodded. Hench was going to be thorough. That's why she'd called him. But God, he was expensive. Where was the money going to come from?

"One last thing," Hench said. "How did the police figure out to charge her?"

Alex sorted through the events. She and Harley had been in town and had just returned when they saw a crowd on shore and some police and other boats out on the lake. An ambulance was parked nearby. Jake Corbett, a neighbour who sometimes visited Harley, had binoculars and was reporting what was happening.

"The boat's DJ's all right. And it looks like DJ that they're trying to revive."

Jake passed Alex the binoculars so she could see.

"What's Jessie doing out there?" Alex's voice was loud even to herself. Harley pulled the binoculars out of her hands.

Harley looked through them for a long time.

"The kid dead or alive?" Elfy asked, bracing herself against Alex's arm.

Alex saw Harley swallow.

"Hard to say."

Horrified, Alex watched as DJ's lifeless body was brought to shore.

"Good, they're putting him on a stretcher, not in a body bag," Elfy whispered beside her. "There's hope." But her voice didn't contain much hope.

After the ambulance sped away, the police boats stayed out on the lake.

"How come Jess isn't coming in?" Elfy asked. There was fear in her voice.

When Jessie did come to shore, her hair was bedraggled from being in the water, and her clothes were sticking to her body, making her look small and thin. Her eyes were down and Alex saw something on Jessie's face she had never seen before: shame.

"The police want me to come down to the station," Jessie said.

Harley moved towards Jessie, but the policemen on either side of her blocked him.

"I'll go with her," Alex said.

The older cop looked at Alex. "I'm sorry ma'am, but—"

"I'm her lawyer," Alex said. "Now get this woman a blanket, or she's not going anywhere." To her surprise, the cop did just that.

At the police station, Jessie blurted out everything before Alex could stop her. She cried as she talked, but held fast to her story that she did not pull the rope.

Alex looked at the police. They had that *nice try but no cigar* look on their faces. It was only a matter of time until Jessie was charged, Alex thought. And if DJ died, she knew what that charge would be: manslaughter.

• • •

Jessie sat with her back against the wall of the teepee. *Don't die, DJ. Don't die.* She said the words over and over again, said them to the stars and moon, to the birds that sang and to the wind itself. Sometimes she went to DJ himself, suspended as he was like a fraying rope bridge between life and death, and whispered the words to him too, filling them with the ferocity of her life force. If only she could bolster him back to life in the same way her breath had done when she'd given him artificial respiration on the lake.

Sometimes, she imagined she could still taste his lips. She had never given mouth to mouth resuscitation before and didn't even know if she'd done it right, but she'd been so desperate to save him, she would have tried anything. After the BANG, she'd rushed out in the boat and found him face down in the water, held up by his life jacket. Jumping in, she pulled him over so he was lying on his back. Her hands were shaking so hard, it was difficult to get them to do what she wanted them to do, but she managed to position him against the jet-ski, then pinched his nose, put her mouth over his and began to exhale into him.

His lungs seemed to take the air and for a wild moment, she thought she might bring him back to life, but as she continued to blow her breath into him, he lay inert in her grasp. She knew she could move her hand to his neck and feel for a pulse, but didn't. If he was dead, she didn't want to know. In fact, the thought of him being dead was so terrifying to her, she gagged and had to stop herself from throwing up.

When the paramedics arrived, they took over, and sometime later, she heard DJ sputter and take his first breath. The sound of it gushed through her body, and she was flooded with relief. She had cried then, the tears hot on her cold face.

She hadn't stopped crying since. Yet, despite the piles of sodden tissues by her side, her body felt wet and spongy, bloated with tears. She felt as if she would cry for the rest of her life.

Was he still alive? Still alive? Still alive? The question

repeated with every beat of her heart. It would be so much easier if she could go to him, be there with him in his hospital room. It would be a relief to minister to his needs and say the prayers she was saying now, but with him closer. She wanted to tell him how sorry she was. Sometimes her yearning to tell him this was so strong, she imagined herself sneaking into his room. But then she'd have to look at him. See his lifeless body. She wouldn't be able to stand that. Besides, his parents would be there and they'd probably chase her away if she got anywhere near him. *Murderer! Murderer!*

She turned her face into the pillow. What had she done? What had she done?

If only she could sleep. She was so tired, so terribly tired, but every time she closed her eyes, the rope was in her hands again and she was pulling it, and there was that awful banging sound and the boat jumping into the air. Then, her arm would thrust out to stop it, to save the boy, but she couldn't save the boy, and there was screaming and crying, most often her own, and she would wake up, so terrified she thought she was going to go out of her mind.

It had been four days since DJ had gone into the coma, and she'd been holed up in the teepee since. She felt frightened to go out, frightened to show her face. In fact, she couldn't imagine ever showing her face again. Aggie, Elfy and the other Grannies wanted to come to her, but she had told Harley to hold them off. At the moment, it was all she could do to breathe. Besides, she wanted to concentrate all her energy on DJ. So hour after hour, she prayed for him, hour after hour she sent him whatever healing energy she could muster.

At other times in her life when she'd done something

she wasn't proud of, she had felt bad, but the feeling was on the periphery of herself like a brown spot on the skin of an apple. Now, however, she felt as if the very core of her was bad. And that everyone now knew that this was so.

She remembered a time when she was eight and at school. Feeling a sudden looseness in her bowels, she was too frightened to risk a run to the washroom, so she'd sat perfectly still, squeezing the muscles of her bum. To her horror, a wetness came into her pants anyway and an awful smell arose around her. The kids pointed and whispered. Trying to cover her mortification, she stared straight ahead, ashamed that what was inside her should be so putrid and awful. Ashamed that she couldn't stop it from coming out.

Shame. It was an emotion her clients often talked about, but it wasn't one she'd had often. Now, she understood more than ever how debilitating it was. Part of her shame was that everyone in town now knew about the rope and the fact that the police had questioned her. They were probably all waiting, as she was, for the police to formally charge her. And here she was, or had been, a respected member of the community. She had disgraced herself and her profession.

How could she have even considered doing what she did to DJ? How could she have been so naïve as to imagine he wouldn't get hurt? All the ranting she'd done over the years about people being in denial and then there she was, in the worst denial of all. There was no excuse for it. Particularly since it had all been laid out in front of her at the sweat: the feather pointing her in the right direction and the image of her mouth on DJ's steering her away from the wrong direction. If only she'd followed the guidance she'd been given.

And now DJ was unconscious. Even if he came out of his coma, there was no certainty he might not be brain damaged, even brain dead. This thought made her retch and she pulled the bowl she'd been using towards her. Dry heaves overtook her. When they finally stopped, she wiped the sweat from her face. Who said Hell was a place you went to, she thought. Hell was right here in this teepee. And it was roasting her alive.

She felt a hand place itself gently on her back.

"It's just me," Harley said.

"Any word?"

Harley sighed. "No."

She knew what that meant. Things were still the same. *Don't die, DJ. Don't die.*

"Well, I called everyone," Harley said. For the last few days he had taken it upon himself to contact her clients and tell them she was taking a leave of absence. He didn't have to call all of them. Some had already cancelled via their answering machine.

"Janice Mitchell says to tell you she's thinking about you. Paul, too."

Jessie's eyes stung. She felt undeserving of their caring.

Harley wiped beneath her eyes with his shirtsleeve. "I'm going to town. Why don't you come for the drive? It would do you good to get out."

Jessie cringed. What if she *saw* someone? What if people recognized her and stared? Or pointed?

Harley read her mind. "You can stay in the car."

Jessie imagined the people gathering around the car now, yelling at her, spitting at the window.

"I can't."

Harley became still. "You can't hide out like this. You're innocent."

Jessie remained silent. Was she? She'd sworn to the police she was. Sworn to Alex, to Hench, to Harley. To anyone and everyone who would listen. But the doubt remained. She'd gone over it a thousand times, felt the rope in her hands, felt herself lifting it. But she hadn't pulled it, had she? Trying to remember was making her crazy. Then, as was happening to her lately, her mind tripped into another reality and suddenly she was sitting in a packed courtroom and a prosecutor was pelting questions at her.

And isn't it true, *Ms* Dearborn, that you *wanted* to stop DJ?

"Yes."

And isn't it true that you *intentionally* tied the rope to the buoy?

"Yes!"

The prosecutor had mirrored sunglasses and was jabbing his finger at her. "You set the rope up so the boy would hit the rocks, and you expect us to believe you didn't pull it?"

Jessie put her face in the pillow. Maybe she did. Maybe she did.

Chapter 15

DJ stared down at his body as he hovered near the hospital room ceiling. He felt light as air. There was a misty white umbilical-like cord attaching him to his physical part that was lying on the bed. The cord was elastic somehow and allowed him to move as close or far away as he wanted. Near the bed, his parents were hunched over the part of him that lay there. He could hear them crying. It made him sad to see his parents upset like this, but he knew he couldn't reach them. He'd already tried.

He thought about going back down the cord and climbing inside his body again, but the pain was awful there. Besides, nothing in his body worked. He couldn't get his lips to open or his fingers to move and until he could, he knew his parents would not be happy.

Although it didn't surprise him that his parents were so upset, he knew it would surprise the comatose part of him on the bed. His parents had always been so busy, so very busy. And now his father was cursing himself for not spending more time, with him swearing that if his son lived, things would be different. Things would be better. There were a lot of people swearing to make changes here in the hospital. Yesterday he'd floated into the intensive care room and could hear the visitors, their wet eyes pressed shut, whispering promises. *Please God, save my husband, daughter, wife...*

In some of these rooms, the Light Ones were there also. Over the last few days, he'd seen many people leave their bodies and waft into their waiting arms. Too bad the people left behind couldn't see what a relief death was. But then they couldn't see the Light Ones, couldn't feel their comforting warmth. He wished he could go with the Light Ones himself. He was getting tired of floating around, not being in one world or the other.

Last night, however, he'd seen something different. A woman left her body and was going towards the Light, but was turned back. And when she'd entered her body again and started breathing again, she was different. She seemed to have some of the Light still around her. He'd heard that after someone had come close to the Light Ones, there was a sort of radiance to them.

Looking at his parents' grieving faces, he wished he could make them understand that the DJ on the bed was only a small part of who he was. And that even if the body on the bed ceased to exist, there was still another part of him, a more enduring part that would go on. Which meant that his parents could never really lose him. But he knew his parents would not believe this even if he was able to whisper it in their ears.

There was something else his parents wouldn't understand, something about the accident, and he was glad they were not aware of it. Hopefully, they never would be aware of it. He didn't want his parents to suffer more. Unfortunately, whether his parents found out or not wasn't up to him. As in all such matters, The Great Order would preside. What would be, would be. But his parents did not know about the Great Order and because of this, he stretched the arms they could not feel around them and held them close.

•   •   •

Needing to get away from the house, Alex went off to look for the field of moss Harley had shown her when she first arrived. She stepped into the forest and stopped, startled at what she saw. Orange 'X's had been spray painted on hundreds of the trees around her. She shuddered and carried on walking. Were all these trees going to be killed? Seeing them all marked like this was eerie. It gave her the creeps.

Obviously, the development project was going ahead after all. This surprised her. With DJ still in a coma, she thought Price would have had more important things on his mind. But the rumour Aggie had told her was that Price wanted Jessie and Harley off the property more than ever, so much so that he'd hired a legal firm that specialized in such things to "take care of the details." They certainly weren't wasting any time.

Seeing an area up ahead that wasn't marked with X's, she headed towards it, then climbed a hill and followed a ridge that looked familiar. Were things ever going to get better? Like everyone else, day after day, she hoped for news of DJ's recovery, but no such news came. She was beginning to think he would never recover. It was such a tragedy. In a way, it didn't matter how it had happened or what had caused it. Neither of those facts would change his condition. She thought of her own son Evan and what it would feel like to peer down into his unconscious face, desperate to see a twitch of life.

It had been nineteen days now. Alex knew because one of the local churches, which had set up a prayer group for DJ, had taken it upon themselves to post the number in big letters on its front door every day. She'd heard that the longer someone was unconscious, the less likely they were to recover with their faculties intact. Was this true? In the last while, she'd heard a hundred things about comas and had no idea if even one of them was right.

Although DJ's state concerned her, she was far more worried about Jessie. The woman was deteriorating before her very eyes. If only Jessie would eat. She was beginning to look like a skeleton covered in cling wrap. Once, a few years ago, a cousin of hers, Janice, had bumped an old man with her car and broken his leg. Although the leg had healed completely within a few weeks, Janice's guilt had been so debilitating that she'd ended up going on anti-depressants for over a year. If breaking someone's leg could cause such remorse, what would it be like to seriously hurt another, perhaps even kill them?

As often as Alex went over the facts, they always led her to the inarguable conclusion that Jessie had pulled the rope. Certainly people in town seemed to think she had. There had been several abusive phone calls and more threats to the loons. But there was a difference between pulling the rope to stop the kid and pulling the rope to hurt the kid. It was that sliver of a difference that she was sure Hench would stretch until he could drive a truck down it. He would argue that Jessie was stressed from the eviction notice, overworked from her selfless work to save birds, sleep-deprived to the point of insanity. He would convince the jury that Jessie was a good woman, a caring, conscientious woman who, in a moment of rage, had made a mistake in judgment. Yes, that mistake had led to a horrible tragedy, but it was certainly not her intention that this be so.

If only they had the results of the forensic investigation. Alex had called down to Hench's office again this morning, but there was still no word on when it would be in. It could be weeks. Meanwhile, with the development project going ahead like this, Jessie and Harley were going to have to find another place to live. Which meant that she and Luke would have to return to the city. What choice was there? Funny, she thought. Even Christina seemed happy about her being in Muskoka now. Jessie pulled a paper from her pocket. It was the drawing Christina had done of the loons. It was lovely.

Unfortunately, if she wanted to remain in Muskoka, she'd have to rent a place and find a job. What kind of work could someone with her qualifications get up here? At this stage in her life, she wasn't willing to work as a teller in a bank. She thought about following up on her mother's offer of financial aid, but discounted it. Knowing how out of touch her mother was with the world, that probably meant a fifty-dollar bill or two. Some help that would be.

She heard a plane overhead and looked up. It was the same seaplane she'd noticed before. Seeing it reminded her of that dream she'd had in the sweat lodge. Even if it was only a hallucination, it had felt so real and so utterly wonderful to fly. She smiled, remembering the way her mother had waved and told her it was all right to fly away. If only that were so. It was ludicrous to think that an experience that happened in a makeshift sauna could be relied upon.

Obviously, the heat in the sweat had impaired her ability to think. With her brain not functioning, she had felt herself dropping down to a kind of knowing place somewhere near her womb. And in that knowing place, she felt as if she could trust the way things were unfolding. In that knowing place, she felt as if she didn't have to work her life, or manipulate it, all she had to do was relax and follow the pulse of her inner wisdom. Of course, now that the sweat was behind her, her rational mind had reinstated itself at the helm of her life and relegated what happened in the ceremony to the irrelevant and fantastical. But, still, it had made her wonder.

She tramped on, trying to mark her whereabouts by remembering certain rocks and trees. Everything looked the same. She climbed a ridge, and when she still didn't know where she was, she decided to turn back. She walked and walked, until she came to another ridge. When she realized it was the same one, her hands began to perspire. Had she gone in a circle? Or did this rocky ridge simply look like the last one?

Worried she was lost, she climbed to the top of a hill to see if the added height would give her some clues. She was breathless by the time she got to the top but could see water. Thank God, she thought and thrashed down towards it. When she was nearer the lake, she could see a small, leaf-green cottage set back on the land. Not seeing anyone around, she knocked on the door. If she could use a phone, she could call Harley and ask him to pick her up. When no one answered, she wandered down to the dock, thinking she might recognize a landmark and be able to walk along the shoreline to Jessie's.

The plane was louder now and was descending

towards the lake. With awe, she watched the plane career
through the air in front of her and slide across the surface
of the water. Oh, my God, it's coming here, she thought,
feeling self-conscious about being on this stranger's dock.
Realizing it would look even worse to leave, she stood
awkwardly and waited as the plane came in. The pilot, a
man with a white beard and ruddy complexion, smiled as
he jutted the upper part of his body through the window.
She recognized him immediately.

"Jake Corbett," she said. She remembered him from
the day of DJ's accident. Jake had been the one to pass her
the binoculars.

"Hello there." He held out a muscular hand.

When she explained she was trying to get back to
Jessie's, he motioned to the seat beside him. "Come on, I'll
take you."

"But—"

"It's faster by plane."

She got in. The plane was small inside, with two seats
and two sets of controls. They put on their seat belts, and
within minutes were off. The engine was loud compared
to any planes Alex had been in before, and it was full of
vibration as it gathered speed. Then, suddenly, the air
seemed to pick it up, and they scudded above the water.
Soon they were high up, gliding like a seagull on a long
scarf of wind. Beneath her, all was lush green and watery
blue.

"It's so beautiful," she said.

"You can say that again. Want a little fly around?"

Alex smiled. "Sure!" She felt a deep feeling of relief to
leave behind all that was on land. She was sick of the
world and happy to fly above it. Hundreds of feet up now,

the plane seemed slower, and she began to feel as if they were floating. An easy contentment moved through her.

"You like flying, don't you?"

Perhaps because she was several hundred feet above the world she normally inhabited and no longer felt constricted by its conventions, she found herself throwing caution to the wind and telling him about her lifelong wish to fly. She told him about the flying dreams she had had as a child and the wings she and her mother had made. She told him about jumping off the back fence in her efforts to be airborne.

"You sound like a woman in need of a plane."

She laughed and the sound of it filled the cockpit. "That's true," she said. "I am a woman in need of a plane." It sounded good to say it.

Jake chuckled, lifted his hands from the controls and intertwined his fingers behind his head. The plane continued its placid movement forward. Alex looked at Jake's hands which were still behind his head. Why wasn't he flying the plane? Her anxiety became more extreme as the minutes passed.

"Shouldn't—shouldn't you be—"

He grinned at her, revealing two button-sized dimples. "Someone should." He nodded to the steering wheel in front of Alex. "Give it a try."

"But I don't know how!"

"From the sound of things, it's time you learned."

•   •   •

From her hideout in Harley's truck, Jessie could see the flowers inside the supermarket. Harley was inside getting groceries. She'd told him she was going to stay in the car and wait for him, but the colours of the flowers drew her into the store. Everyone at home kept telling her how thin she was, but if she was so thin, why did her body feel so heavy?

The flowers looked like they belonged to another world, not the dull, grey one she inhabited. Should she buy some? Send them to DJ? She yearned to do something for him. The idea of being able to put something in his room that had colour and life would ease some of her anguish. She stood in front of the daffodils. They were too yellow. Trumpeted too much cheer. She looked at the roses. They were the colour of dried blood. She didn't want to think about blood in any form. Maybe she should buy white flowers—there were some white chrysanthemums there. But chrysanthemums were what you saw at a funeral. She steadied herself. The thought of a funeral made her want to throw up again.

"Can I help you?"

A saleswoman with chapped lips appeared in front of her.

Jessie felt as if she had to reach down and drag her voice up her throat, like she might drag a frightened animal from a tunnel. "I don't know."

"What's the occasion?"

Jessie stood motionless like a deer caught in headlights. "Occasion" was definitely not the right word. What could she say? Boy on deathbed? Was there a card for that? It was odd how dark one's humour could become in a dark time. Seeing some plants, she mumbled something and wandered over to the display. Maybe a plant would be better. A plant had roots and would live longer. That way, if, no, *when,* DJ woke up from his coma, there might be something to look at.

If Jessie could have, she would have sent flowers to the entire town. "I'm sorry," she wanted to say to each and every person. She felt particularly bad when she thought about The Grannies. For as DJ lay in the hospital fighting for life, the Save Wildwood campaign passed away as quickly as a person deprived of oxygen. Their hope of saving the Wildwood property was now irrevocably lost. Their only chance had been to create an avalanche of opposition from the community and there was no possibility of that now. The whole town was focussed on DJ and his survival. And it should be, she thought.

Forcing herself to choose a plant, Jessie picked one with glossy leaves and a white flower and took it to the sales woman.

"A peace plant," the woman said, wrapping it up.

Jessie nodded dully. She hadn't known the plant's name, but liked that it had the word "peace" in it. For it *was* a peace offering. It felt a little bit like tossing a thimble of water into a conflagration, but nonetheless, she had to do something. Apparently, many people in town felt the same way because rumour had it that Price and his wife had received an avalanche of flowers and cards.

She had received some cards too. One said, "If DJ dies, you're next." Another had a picture of Jesus nailed to the cross and promised that if Jessie accepted Christ as her personal redeemer, she would be saved. Saved from her sins maybe, but obviously not the anger of the townspeople. Some of the townspeople, Harley reminded her.

The saleswoman rang up the purchase. Moving

deliberately so her hands stayed steady, Jessie paid for the plant and wrote out the delivery information. As she was walking away, the saleswoman called to her.

"You forgot to write down who they're from—"

Jessie turned and fled as fast as her weak legs would carry her.

•   •   •

Alex was in the bird room cleaning cages. She was spending a lot of time in the bird room lately. Not that there were many birds. There hadn't been a new admission for weeks. But still, there were birds to take care of and she and Elfy were sharing the work between them.

Alex worked quickly. Jake was flying over to Parry Sound this morning, and if she got her work done here, she planned to go with him. Every time she went up with him, he let her fly. And today he was going to show her how to land. If she learned how to land, he said he just might let her take the plane up for a spin around the lake by herself one day. She was hoping she'd know how to do this by the time Tom came again. She wanted to show him what she could do.

Her thoughts were interrupted by the sound of someone coming down the stairs and she turned to see Elfy. Of all Jessie's friends, Elfy was taking what had happened to Jessie the hardest. The old woman seemed continually anxious and out of sorts. Since Harley was staying out in the teepee with Jessie and the boys were sleeping outside in a tent near the loons, the old woman was staying at the house now. Elfy felt someone should be near the bird room at night, especially since they'd had more threats. But did Elfy ever sleep? Alex could hear Elfy pacing the floor at all times of the night. Sometimes Alex could hear her talking, prattling on as if she was trying to convince someone of something. To Alex, it sounded like mumbled gibberish.

"Heard anything?" Elfy asked, sitting heavily on a stool beside Alex.

Alex winced. If she was asked this question one more time she was going go scream. "You'd be the first to know."

"How's Jess? You see her?"

"No."

"Listen, I've been wondering," Elfy said. "How much is that bigwig lawyer costing anyway?"

Alex set a cage down and shrugged. She didn't want to say anything until she and Hench had come to an agreement. If all went well, she might be able to trade off some of his legal services for financial advice. After all, she didn't have to have an office downtown to do that. If she couldn't cover the fees that way, she was going to talk to her mother.

"It hasn't been decided yet," Alex said, looking at the old woman. Worry had slashed more lines on Elfy's face.

"The kid could be in a coma for years, for crying out loud. I read of a case where—"

Alex tuned the old woman out. Although she still hoped that DJ would recover, she was getting to the point where she wanted him either to get better or pass away. This in-between place was like being tied to a rock in the middle of nowhere. She couldn't imagine how difficult it must be for DJ's parents. At least if the kid died, everyone could mourn and move on. The way it was now was living hell.

Unable to stand Elfy's rant for one minute longer, she

put her hand on the old woman's arm. "It will be all right," she said firmly. "Hench will make it all right."

Elfy's worry lines deepened. "I hope so. I don't want her going to jail!"

Alex sighed. "I wouldn't count on her *not* going to jail. But, even if she does, it won't be for long. And she'll get time off for good behaviour." She knew from Elfy's agitation that she'd said the wrong thing.

"Maybe I should talk to Hench."

Alex groaned. That was all he needed! Elfy phoning him and jabbering on about the case. "I think we should just leave him to do what he has to do." She checked her watch. Very soon she'd be up in the air, flying as far away as Jake would let her.

"But what if there was new information?"

Alex looked at Elfy. "What do you mean, 'new information'?"

"What if it turned out that the person who everybody thought pulled the rope, *wasn't* the person who pulled the rope?"

Alex felt herself soften. She knew Elfy would do just about anything to have Jessie's name cleared. She remembered her lawyer friends regaling each other with stories about what the family and friends of their clients would do to get their loved ones off the hook.

"There would have to be proof. Irrefutable proof," Alex said.

"Would a confession work?"

Alex raised her eyebrows. "A confession? Of course a confession would work. A confession would change everything." She looked at Elfy hard. "Elfy, if you have information, reliable information—"

There was a honk outside. Alex stood up. As soon as she did, Elfy shoved a paper on the table.

"Here, watch me sign this." Elfy pulled out a pen and wrote her name on the bottom of the paper.

Alex gave the typed pages a quick glance. "What is it? A will?"

Elfy nodded. "With all the threats going on, I thought I should have one. Here, sign it." She held out the pen.

Alex looked outside. It was Jake all right. "Oh, Elfy, let's do this later when—"

Elfy put the pen in her hand. "Take two secs."

Alex picked up the pen, and with great gravity, witnessed Elfy's signature. Then she rushed out. She had an airplane waiting.

•   •   •

When Jessie came out of the house, she saw the dead loon sprawled on the screen over the top of the pool and screamed. The boys scrambled out of their tent and screamed too. As if from out of nowhere, Harley charged towards them, then seeing what they were screaming about, stopped and stood perfectly still, staring at the carcass. Very slowly, he moved forward and picked up the dead loon. He laid it carefully on the ground, then lifted the screen off the pool.

"It's all right," he called. "Sushi and Gumption are all right."

Seeing the two loons huddled at one end of the pool, Jessie put her arm around Evan. The boy looked as if he was going to be sick. Her own heart was pounding.

Harley took the carcass of the dead loon into the

woods. When he returned, he was hefting a canoe. "I'm getting the loons out of here."

He'd been talking for a while now about taking them to an isolated lake where his cousin had a cabin. "We'll take Sushi today and Gumption later this week." His eyes were on her now. "I'll take the boys, but we'll need you for the first day or so."

Jessie nodded. Other than the trip into town with Harley last week, she hadn't been off the property. But hiding out in the teepee wasn't going to help DJ, and it didn't feel good to leave all the work with the birds to the others. The very thought of being away from the house filled her with guilty pleasure. She went into the house to pack some food while Harley tied the canoe and kayak on top of his truck. When she had it all ready, she told Elfy and Alex, who came out and helped pack up the car.

"I'll help with the first twenty-four hours," Jessie told them, "then drive back tomorrow." She got in beside Harley. In the back seat, the boys were on either side of a large cage that held Sushi. She looked over at Gumption, who was still in the pool. Alex was giving him a minnow, but he did not look happy.

They sped north up the highway. Jessie caught herself wishing they could just keep driving and go as far as the car would take them. What she would have given to leave the life she was living behind.

A few miles north, Harley turned off on a side road which meandered around a farm. Jessie saw some children running between huge spools of hay in the fields.

All the sun long, it was running, it was lovely, the hay fields high as the house, the tunes from the chimneys, it was air and playing, lovely and watery...

The words soothed her, reminded her of times when life hadn't been so difficult. They turned down a narrow road, and Sushi squawked as the truck rocked up and down over the ruts and potholes. They went up a steep incline and suddenly the lake was before them. Rock Lake was small and had only óne cottage on it, the one belonging to Harley's cousin. This cottage would provide a place to sleep as well as shelter from the rain if the weather got bad.

They unloaded everything from the car, then went down to the lake. It was calm, which was a relief. They did not want Sushi buffeted by big waves his first time on the lake.

"Is Sushi going to fly?" Evan asked as he carried the cage down to the water.

"Not today," Harley said, "but soon."

Jessie knew Harley was hoping that one day Sushi would not only fly, but migrate. The experts said this wouldn't happen, but Sushi had flown past every prediction made so far, so it was possible he would soar past this one as well.

Jessie carried the cooler of minnows down to the water, and Harley put the boats in, then climbed in the canoe. Luke climbed in the kayak. When both boats were a few feet out, they positioned them to make a barrier. Then Harley nodded at Jessie.

The time had come. Evan opened the cage door, and Jessie reached in and set Sushi down on the ground a few inches from the water. She looked at Harley. They had worked hard for this moment. The smile felt odd on her face. It had been so long.

Awed by the immensity of the scene before him, Sushi

stood perfectly still for several moments, then waddled toward the lake. As soon as his feet had water under them, he plonked himself down and glided along the clear surface as gracefully as a ball on a glass table. Everyone cheered.

"Must be a shock to find out there's more to life than a swimming pool," Jessie said. She could feel the bird's excitement and was excited herself.

Seeing how well Sushi was handling things, Luke brought the kayak into shore, and Evan climbed in the front hole. Jessie got in the canoe with Harley. Slowly, they began to go further out, a boat on either side of Sushi. Jessie fed the loon minnows so that he wouldn't venture too far off. Harley scanned the sky for predatory birds.

Sushi kept scooting ahead of the canoe, making Jessie nervous. "Stay close," she told him. Like any youngster, he was testing the limits. Jessie made herself relax. Then Sushi did a fateful thing: he took a dive. One moment Jessie saw his tail feathers up-ended in the air, the next moment there were only bubbles.

Jessie held her breath and watched the surface, waiting for Sushi's head to pop up again. She knew he could stay down a long time and that his powerful webbed feet could paddle him a long distance under water. In the pool at home, the sides of it contained him. But here, there was no containment. Then she realized something else. In the pool, the water was clear. The sides were easy to see. The water in the lake, however, was murky and went on for miles. Sushi wasn't prepared for this. The minute he went under water, he wouldn't know where he was.

Quickly, Harley and Jessie paddled out to the middle of the lake where they'd be more visible. They waited for Sushi to surface, but Sushi did not surface.

"Oh, Harley…" She couldn't take this!

"There!" Luke shouted.

Jessie yanked herself around. About a hundred yards away she caught a glimpse of Sushi's head. He looked around frantically, and not seeing them, dove again. They dug their paddles into the water and sped to where he'd gone under. They waited. And waited. And waited.

• • •

Knowing Sushi could be anywhere, they paddled all the way up one side of the lake, then, slowly, made their way back. A wind came up and now there were small waves coming towards them that not only made paddling harder, but also made it extremely difficult to scan the surface of the lake. After a while, Jessie's arms and back ached.

She put down her paddle and rubbed her stinging eyes. They felt scraped raw from the sharp glint of the sun on the water.

"If we don't find him, he'll die," Luke cried. "He can't feed himself. Can't fend off predators…"

Harley put his finger to his lips and shook his head in a "don't go there" gesture. They continued paddling, circling the lake a second time. Harley made his special loon call, sent it out over the water, but only the sound of the waves buffeting the canoes came back.

No one spoke. In the quiet, various scenarios went through Jessie's mind. She saw the sharp-toothed jaws of a turtle grabbing Sushi's leg, yanking him underwater. Then, she saw a hawk grabbing him with his talons. Her mind was like a movie projector, throwing out image after horrendous image, and she couldn't get it to stop.

This time as they went around the lake, Harley steered the canoe closer to shore. There was a slim chance that Sushi, exhausted from swimming, might have climbed up on land. Since loons don't walk well, they both knew if Sushi was on shore, he wouldn't be far from the water. Nevertheless, because the colours of the rocks and reeds were similar to the colours of a loon, he'd be extremely difficult to spot.

Because they were so tired and disheartened, it took them hours to get around the lake again. By the time they neared where they had started, the daylight was running out. They had to find him before dark. He'd never survive a night on his own.

Jessie could barely paddle now. There was a sharp pain in her shoulder every time she moved her arm forward. And that ache was back in her chest. How could she take one more thing going wrong? She looked up ahead and saw the little dock where they'd started from. Once they reached it, it would be all over.

"Harley, look!" Luke pointed like an arrow to the sandy beach. It could be anything, moss, a clump of grass, but they paddled in quickly and beached the boats. Harley got there first and picked up the bird's inert body.

"Minnow. Quick."

Evan raced to the canoe and came back panting. Harley held the minnow in front of Sushi's beak and spoke to him softly in Ojibway.

Sushi's eyes bolted open. He chirped and shat at the same time. Harley laughed and the sound of Harley's laughter seemed to release Sushi from the clutch of his terror, for after a few minutes, he gulped down the minnow as if he'd never expected to eat one again.

· · ·

At first DJ had thought it was kind of cool travelling around wherever he wanted and listening in on people's conversations, but it was boring not being able to talk to anyone. Deciding it was time for his daily check-in, he travelled down the umbilical cord to his physical body and slipped back into it. Pain exploded through him. It wasn't just physical pain. It was the emotional pain of dread. The dread of the Truth coming out. Not that he could stop it. Truth was a powerful force and he knew he could do little to prevent it from finding its way into the Light.

He tried to move his hands. For a moment, he thought his index finger might move, but he was wrong. Then he tried his toes and when he had no success, he slipped out of his body again and hovered a few feet above the bed. He watched his parents come into the room. Their bodies were wooden with grief. He wished the part of him that was in the coma on the bed could see the love in his parents' eyes. Even if the Truth did come out, there was nothing to fear. But the part of him on the bed did fear.

If only the Light Ones would appear again. Yesterday, they had come close, so close he had felt their warth. He was encouraged they were around, for he knew they only came when a crossover was imminent. He was eager to leave now. He wanted more of that radiant peace he'd felt when they were near. If he'd had his way, he would have left with them yesterday, but just when he thought they were going to take him, their light had dimmed and they were gone. He hoped they'd be back. When they were, he was determined to go with them.

In preparation, he began untying some of the strings that connected DJ to the people in his life. There were so many. Some of the strings were vibrating with a slow, reverential kind of energy, and he knew these were attached to people who were praying for his body to recover. But there was one string that had a particularly strange feeling to it, so he followed it along until he came to an old woman. She was writing his name.

He didn't understand why this woman was writing his name, and he didn't have to understand. What mattered was that the words she was writing around his name were not the truth. Would the people who read the letter know this?

He watched as the old woman signed the letter and dated it. Then, she began to put little round things in her mouth. As she did this, he saw the egg of energy encasing her body begin to weaken. Within a few minutes, her aura became limp and grey, just like those other ones had before crossing over to the Light. But something was different. Something was not right. This woman was forcing her death. Making it happen with her will. Could a person override The Great Order with their own will? He thought so, but he wasn't sure. Besides, wouldn't there be consequences?

To save her from whatever those consequences might be, he tried to talk to her, but, as with all those in the physical world, he could not make contact. He watched her swallow pill after pill. He drew back and searched the house to see if there was anyone who might come to the woman's aid. In the lower part of the house, he discovered a woman sleeping. He felt relieved she was sleeping, for he knew that the veils between the worlds thinned when a person was in the dream state, and wondered if it might be possible to penetrate her psyche and contact her. He tried that now, tried to reach into her dream time, but she did not stir. Then he remembered a word, a word that was like a key in the human world, and he shouted that word now.

"Help!"

The woman opened her eyes.

Chapter 16

A lex picked apart her Styrofoam coffee cup until it was no more than a pile of white rubble on the Formica table. She hadn't wanted the coffee but had forced herself to drink it. She had to wake up. At least enough to drive home. It had been a very long night. Thank God Elfy was going to live.

"That number of pills should have put her ten feet under," the doctor had said. "You caught her in the nick of time."

That much Alex was aware of. God, when she'd found Elfy, empty pill bottle in hand, there had barely been a pulse. She yawned. Knowing she was too tired to drive home, she'd come down here to the cafeteria for a cup of coffee to wake herself up. She checked her watch. Five a.m.

She put her head down and closed her eyes. Was Elfy going to be mad at her for spoiling her suicide attempt? Alex could hardly have acted differently. It was pure luck that she'd done anything at all. She still found it incredible that she'd woken up like that. What a relief that she had. And if she hadn't? No, she wouldn't think about it, she told herself. The point was, Elfy was alive. Alive. And she had been the one to save her. It gave Alex a strange feeling of redemption that this had turned out to be so. It made up somehow for what she hadn't been able to do for Lucy.

When she jerked awake sometime later, Jessie was sitting across from her, her eyes as sad as sadness itself.

"Have you seen her?"

Jessie shook her head. "Thanks for calling me."

"I knew you'd want to know."

Jessie nodded. "Lucky I had the cell phone with me."

"She's going to live," Alex said. "Thank God."

"I know. I called the hospital right after you called me."

They both looked at each other tiredly. Finally Jessie spoke. "We seem destined to meet in hospitals, you and I."

Alex managed a small smile. "At least this time, no one died." She frowned, thinking of Lucy.

"Close, though, from what the doctor said."

"Too close."

"But why suicide?" Jessie shook her head. "I don't understand."

Alex could see the pain and confusion on Jessie's face and reached for the paper she'd found in Elfy's hand. She watched as Jessie read the confession.

Jessie looked up with moist eyes. "She was trying to save *me?*" She pushed the paper away as if she didn't want it anywhere near her.

"She thought by giving up her life and confessing to pulling the rope, you could have yours back again. It was an act of love." Her last words surprised her.

Jessie pulled a napkin from the dispenser and dabbed her eyes. "Goodness, will there ever be a day when I don't cry?"

Alex took the paper, folded it and put it back in her purse.

The smell of bacon was beginning to fill the air. Over

on the far side of the room, Alex could see people lining up for breakfast and recognized two of them. She brought her eyes quickly back to Jessie. "Price and his wife are over there."

Jessie sighed and stared at her hands. "I just think things can't get any harder, and then they get harder."

•   •   •

Jessie walked along the corridor. She'd just been in to see Elfy. The old woman had obviously been given some sleeping medication; she was in a dead sleep. Jessie kissed the old woman's forehead and, deciding to come back later, made her way through the hospital corridors. Then suddenly she stopped and stood staring at a certain door. How she had known to stop there she had no idea, but she was sure she was standing in front of DJ's room.

Here it was, the opportunity she'd been waiting for, and she was terrified. Given that she'd just seen DJ's parents starting breakfast, she knew she had about twenty minutes. But what if there was a nurse in the room? If there was, she could simply back out again. She put her moist palm against the door and pushed gently. Except for the boy, the room was empty.

At first she thought she had the wrong room; the person lying on the bed looked so young and innocent. His hair had been cut short, and the skin on his face looked soft, almost fragile. The impact of seeing him this close was too much for her. She fell into the chair that had been pulled up close to his bed.

The stillness of his body horrified her. Was he breathing? Sadness spilled out of her, and she put her head on the bed near his comatose hand and cried. As her tears fell, she told him she hadn't meant for him to get hurt, not like this, and that she wanted him to get better. She told him that she no longer knew if she had pulled the rope or not, but if she had, she was sorry. She repeated the word sorry over and over until her throat was sore. Then, when there were no more words, a deep, anguished crying erupted out of her. She thought she was going to cry forever when she felt a hand move, as if in comfort.

• • •

Alex stared at the front page of the local newspaper. There on the front was DJ's smiling face. The kid looked so different. Yes, he still had the red hair and freckles, but his whole demeanor was different. Fair enough, she thought. The kid had just walked into a whole new life. She spent a few moments reading the story. Although DJ was still in the hospital, according to these reports, he was able to do more each day. His doctors had done various tests and were quoted as saying they expected DJ's complete recovery. Alex was glad.

Things were starting to move. She could feel it. The feeling was so strong in her body that she wasn't surprised when later in the day the phone rang and it was Hench's secretary saying the forensic report was in. Alex told her to fax it to the local office supply place, then raced into town to get it, driving so fast that the fax was still being transmitted when she arrived. Luckily for her, the saleswoman wasn't busy and passed the first page to her as it came through.

She whistled as she read, not trusting herself to talk.

Then, worried that she'd tipped the saleswoman off that something newsworthy was being transmitted, she forced herself to make conversation so the woman wouldn't peek at the pages as they came in. My God. The newspapers would have a field day if they got hold of this. And they might get hold of it. But only if she wanted them to. She was going to have to play this very carefully.

•   •   •

Jessie wandered amongst the marked trees. She was here to say goodbye. Tomorrow at this time, all this beauty would be gone. Sometimes, she speculated that people in urban environments were intrigued with clothes and fancy cars and holidays because they were trying to get their need for beauty fulfilled. Goodness, if she lived in the city and was surrounded by concrete boxes, she'd have a need to buy herself some beauty too. To her, beauty was a soul need.

As she walked, she tried to estimate the number of trees that would be coming down. A few thousand, at the very least. She searched out the trees that didn't have orange bands, the trees that, for landscaping or aesthetic reasons, were being allowed to live. Over the large acreage, she found seven or eight copses of trees that weren't marked for destruction and tried to be grateful for them.

The problem was, after she'd had a few days of incredible relief, she'd allowed herself to get hopeful. After DJ had come out of his coma, she'd let herself hope that Price might feel more magnanimous towards them and be willing to negotiate. She'd called him twice, hoping to talk to him, but he hadn't called back.

Jessie grazed her open palm on the trunk of a young

beech tree. Its bark was as smooth as soft leather. Then she let her fingers flutter through some pine fronds. They felt silky. It was strange to her that more people didn't value the life of this forest. To her, it was alive, green and intelligent. Yet, to most of the population, it was considered expendable and unimportant. DJ's life, on the other hand, was presumed to have great value. Hundreds of dollars had been spent to keep him alive. Which was as it should be, because human life was precious, but why wasn't this forest considered precious, too?

Jessie wondered for a moment if she should chain herself to one of the trees and repeat the protest she'd done a few years ago when another stand of trees had been threatened. But last time there had been a chance of saving them. There hadn't been a dozen machines ready to roll and another dozen men ready to chainsaw. Nevertheless, it would feel good to have the trees know that at least one person had taken a stand for them. If she rooted around, she would probably be able to find a bicycle chain somewhere. Hadn't she seen one yesterday when she and the boys were packing up the basement?

The poor boys. They looked so unhappy. Specially Evan.

"You can come visit," Jessie had said to him.

"I don't *want* to visit," he said, his eyes full of longing. "I want to live here."

Jessie didn't say any more to him. She understood how he felt. She would have been miserable living away from nature, too.

By the end of the day, they'd had most of their things packed. The majority of boxes were going into storage. There wasn't room for much at the little cabin on the lake where Harley had taken the loons, but it would be perfect for her and Harley and Luke, at least until they knew what their next step was. Her plan was to move there as soon as the first tree came down. She wasn't going to stay around and watch. That would be too painful. But now, just for a moment, she thought about whether to make a last protest. As she was considering this, she heard someone calling.

•   •   •

"I've been looking for you everywhere," Alex called as she pulled the car over to the side of the road. "Come on, get in!" When Jessie did, she gunned the car and headed towards the hospital.

"What's going on? Tell me!"

"The forensic report. I've got it. " She glanced at Jessie. "Don't look so scared."

"Nothing but scary things have been happening for the last month, and you're telling me not to be scared? Where are we going?"

"To the hospital. I want Elfy to hear this at the same time."

Parking the car illegally, she grabbed Jessie's arm and they hurried towards Elfy's room. They found the bed empty.

"Where the heck is she?" Alex said. After Elfy had had her stomach pumped, she'd developed an infection in her throat that had spread to her lungs, and she'd been put on oxygen. Knowing how precarious a person's health could be at Elfy's age, Alex flagged down a nurse and asked if she knew where Elfy was.

"Try the sunroom," the nurse said affably.

Alex and Jessie walked quickly down the hall. As they approached the sunroom, Alex slowed their pace. Looking past the back of one of the wing chairs she could see a young boy playing cards.

"Is that DJ?" Alex whispered. Again, she had the feeling that who she was seeing was different from the boy who had sneered at her that day on the Wildwood dock. Where had all that surliness gone?

DJ looked up from his cards as they approached.

Alex noticed the oxygen canister by the other chair.

"Elfy!" Jessie said, before Alex could.

Elfy's small hand waved them in. "Hi, you guys! I'm skunking this kid."

"You wish," DJ said, playing a card.

For several minutes the only sound was the shuffling of cards. "Takes a lot to beat me," Elfy said.

DJ nodded. "Yeah."

The two women stood awkwardly, watching DJ and Elfy play. Alex could feel Jessie's anxiety and cleared her throat.

"I've got the forensic report."

Elfy's eyes shot up to Jessie. Her face was full of apprehension. "What's it say?" DJ moved to get up, but Elfy waved him down. "Stay! You're gonna hear it sooner or later anyway."

Alex cleared her throat and pulled the report from the envelope.

Elfy adjusted the tube of oxygen that ran beneath her nose as if making certain the supply was going to continue to be available. Jessie sat down and braced herself.

Alex wasted no time. She didn't bother reading from

the report. She knew what it said. "I'll summaraize," she said. "They found no trace of rock on the bottom of the jet-ski. But they did find paint. That means that the jet-ski hit the buoy, not the rocks."

DJ bit his lip and swallowed.

Alex continued. "So, it wasn't DJ hitting the rocks that caused the accident." She looked at Jessie and saw the wetness rimming her eyes.

Elfy looked at DJ. "You hit the buoy? What made you do that?"

The question hung in the silence. A booming voice broke into the quiet.

"What's going on here?"

They all turned. Dick Price strode into the room and stood protectively by his son.

Seeing the dangerous look in his eyes, Alex said, "We should go." There was more to this report that she knew Price wouldn't like.

DJ reached for his father's hand. "Dad, they have a forensic report..."

"I don't care what they have. I won't listen to a word, not without my lawyer!"

DJ took a slow breath. When he spoke, his voice was soft. "Dad, don't..."

Alex watched Price carefully. Yes, she could see the man's aggressive protectiveness, but she could also see the love he had for his son. Good thing, she thought. Because the real bomb of this report had yet to explode.

"Perhaps your father would like to read the report himself," Alex said. She placed the papers on the table. As she suspected, Price was not able to resist picking them up.

They all watched as he scanned the page, his face

reddening. "This is ridiculous! DJ wouldn't have hit a *buoy*. He knows how to drive a boat!"

Alex knew that the part that was going to make Price apoplectic was about three-quarters of the way down the page. She watched his eyes race through the print, then stop and swell with outrage.

"DJ! This—tell me this isn't—"

Keeping her voice neutral, Alex explained to the others. "According to the report, on the day of the accident, DJ's blood showed significant traces of Ecstasy, a drug with the same mind-bending hallucinogenic abilities as LSD." It was no wonder he'd hit the buoy. With a drug like that inside him, the world must have been spinning like a merry-go-round.

Price put a hand on his son's shoulders and shook him, as if trying to shake free the words of denial he so needed to hear. When he saw DJ wince in pain, he dropped his hands, stepped back and collapsed into a chair. The report fell from his hands, its pages splaying on the floor. With dead eyes, he turned to Alex.

"Who knows about this?"

Here it was, the leverage she'd been waiting for.

"No one," Alex said. "And no one will. Provided we are able to agree on certain conditions."

• • •

Up ahead of their canoe, Sushi flew with graceful ease. It thrilled Jessie to watch him. She felt like a proud parent, relishing in the abilities of her offspring. Sushi knew how to take care of himself now, feeding and flying with the same abilities as any loon his age. He was nearly all grown up. Any day now, they expected him to migrate. As Harley said, there was no reason for him not to migrate. It was what he knew how to do.

Summer was all but over now. The sun was sinking into the lake earlier in the evening, and there was an autumn mist curling on the surface of the water in the mornings. Jessie looked up. The sky was such a startling, definite blue, she thought if she reached her arm over her head, her fingers would come back as blue as if she'd dipped them in paint. A V of geese was flying at the far end of the lake. They were gathering, getting ready for their arduous journey south. Was the goose they'd found with the arrow in its neck among them? It would be an extraordinary coincidence, but why not? It had been a summer of miracles. But it had also been a summer of misery, and she was ready to leave it all behind her. Besides, she had something special to look forward to.

Ahead of them, she watched as Gumption did a face plant into the water again. It was difficult to watch his relentless attempts to fly. If grit and determination had been enough, Gumption would have been airborne by now. Jessie watched as he flapped his wings as hard as he could to get up speed. With only one foot to stabilize him, however, he began to wobble, then, SPLASH! He hit the water once again.

"It's pathetic," she said to Harley.

"Got that right."

They had both agonized about whether to bring Gumption out to the lake. There was a zoo in Toronto that wanted him, and thinking that being in a zoo was as good a life as a one-footed loon was going to get, they'd arranged to take him there. But, in the end, they hadn't been able to make themselves do it and had brought him to the lake instead. They would let nature decide.

So far, however, it had been a frustrating experience for Gumption. He was exhausting himself trying to do something he was simply not capable of doing. They shouldn't have brought him.

Across the water, she could hear the kids shrieking. When she'd left them, Luke and Evan were about to go swimming. From the sounds of it, they'd just jumped in. Jessie touched the water. The lake was much cooler than it had been even a few days ago. A few cold nights was all it took. Luke was already counting the number of swims he had left.

After this weekend, the boys would return to school. It wasn't going to be easy getting either boy into shoes and underwear and socks. Jessie felt so grateful they had been able to spend the summer here with the lake and trees and birds. If wilderness was going to be protected, people had to know about it and experience it. Thanks to the birds, the boys had a firm respect for it now. It ran inside their bodies, warm as blood.

Hopefully, that respect would be fostered in more children now that the Wildwood Nature Reserve was about to become a reality. The renovations to Wildwood Lodge were going to begin next week. She and Harley had been over at the lodge every day, talking over the various changes they were going to make. She felt excited, like a bird hopping on a branch before its first flight.

They had decided to make as few changes to Wildwood as possible. As a nature retreat, the place would still need most of the same facilities, but if they were going to have groups of school children visit, which was their plan, they needed to extend the kitchen. Luckily for them, Price had sold them the lodge for such a reasonable amount that they had enough funds left to make these changes as well as to pay for a director.

Thank goodness for Alex. First of all, she'd handled nearly all the negotiations with Price. Not that the man had made it difficult. In fact, he seemed almost eager to be rid of the place in the end. His secretary had told the cook, who told Aggie, who told Jessie, that all Dick Price wanted to do these days was spend time with his son. Fair enough, thought Jessie. He'd almost lost DJ. It pleased her to hear he was taking full advantage of his second chance.

She felt as if she were getting a second chance too. She now knew in the centre of her being, that it was not her job to monitor another person's actions. Not if those actions were legal anyway. Yes, she would continue to fight for what she believed in, but she would not step onto the sacred ground of another person's choices. She smiled. DJ had taught her this. And to think she'd imagined that she was going to teach him a lesson. You could never always sometimes tell how things were going to work out.

She never would have guessed, for example, that Alex would turn out to be such a central figure in the buying of Wildwood. The woman had been incredible. Once she'd negotiated with Price about selling the property and had the finances figured out, she'd managed to do something even more extraordinary: she'd found a benefactor. At the moment, that benefactor wished to remain anonymous, but Alex told Jessie that when the renovations were completed, she hoped to persuade this person to visit. Sensing Alex's awkwardness, Jessie had not pressed for more information. Alex would tell her what she needed to tell her in her own time.

Meanwhile, Jessie was enjoying getting to know Alex's family more. She still hadn't met Alex's father, but she was talking to Shirley Lockhart, Alex's mother, regularly. It had felt a bit odd doing therapy over the phone, and Jessie had been reluctant at first, but Alex had asked her specially, and she felt it was the least she could do. Already the woman was opening up. It always filled Jessie with wonder to watch someone reach an arm through the prison bars of their patterns. It reminded Jessie of that saying she used to have on her office wall: *And finally the day will come when the risk it takes to remain tight inside the bud will be more painful than the risk it takes to blossom.*

Of everyone, the person who was happiest right now was Evan. Dear Evan. Did he even know where his puffer was anymore? It would be great if he could move into his new house without it. How were they going to fit into that tiny place? Jessie only hoped Alex's decision was going to work. It was one thing to visit for a few weeks, but an entirely different matter to live in Muskoka all year. As delighted as Evan was, she didn't think Tom was pleased with the idea. But he and Christina would come up weekends, or Alex and Evan would go down there. It was a bit fractured, Jessie had to admit, but fractured was better than broken, and she'd seen families survive worse arrangements. Meanwhile, Alex would carry on flying. The woman had a passion now, and that wasn't to be ignored.

The move was going to take place next weekend. Maggie, the woman who had started the bird refuge, had already come back and taken the last of her things. Poor

Maggie. Her mother's heart was still bad, and Maggie had
decided to move out to Alberta to take care of her. It was
ironic, Jessie thought, how one door closed and another
door opened.

It wouldn't take her and Harley long to transfer the
last of the bird things to their house. Now that she was
going to be a full-time bird woman, she thought she'd
better get organized and have all the equipment in one
place. She had a lot to learn and it would take her a long
time to know half of what Maggie did, but Elfy and
Harley would help. Besides, there was a visceral eagerness
within her to go forward into this next phase of her life.
So, she was going to spread her wings and jump off the
branch of all she had known and fly into the wind.

•   •   •

Alex let the plane drop in altitude so that she was just
above the lakes and trees. She could almost count the ice
cubes in people's drinks. She liked to fly this low. It made
her feel part of the world, yet not part of it at the same
time. It was a beautiful day, warm and lush.

Beside her, Corbett was having a nap. What
confidence he had in her! She looked over at him fondly.
How extraordinary that their two lives had intersected. He
was like a father to her, supporting her in ways her own
father had never been able to. And now, here he was,
teaching her to fly. Sometimes she asked questions and
when she did, he was happy to instruct her, but often, like
today, all she wanted was to be quiet and absorb the sound
of the wind and the burning blue of sky.

Down below she could see the black smoke from the

steamboat, the Seguin, as it voyaged towards Port Carling. Several smaller boats were following it, criss-crossing its wake. She followed the steamboat and as it neared the town, saw the wooden barriers lower across the road to stop traffic. A line of cars began to pile up behind the barrier. Then, the huge bridge began to jack-knife into the air. It was awesome, watching as thousands of pounds of bolts and metal rose into the sky. It seemed impossible. But flying an airplane seemed impossible too. And here she was, doing it.

The line of cars was longer now, and her eye caught sight of a black Jaguar about twenty cars back. She smiled, imagining that there was a woman in that car, a woman like the one she had been once, drumming her fingers on the steering wheel, cursing the fact that she was going to have to wait fifteen minutes. The woman probably had a briefcase full of important papers lying open on the passenger seat. She might be on her cell phone already, determined to make use of this *unproductive* time by catching up on her calls. For in that woman's world, there was never a moment to be lost. But there was never a moment to be found either. Never a moment just to be.

Alex had many such moments now. In the last year, her life had completely changed. Soon, it would change more. Living up here and being the director of The Wildwood Nature Reserve was going to be an incredible challenge. But then, she always did like a good challenge. And she would be able to continue flying. One day, she might even buy her own plane. Jake said he had one in a hanger down south he'd sell her. She'd have to tell her mother that the next time they talked. Her mother would be pleased.

Was it crazy to think her mother might get better? There was no denying that her mother hadn't stepped out of the house for years, but if her own life could change, then surely her mother's could. And Jessie was working with her now. If anyone could help, she knew Jessie could. Besides, her mother couldn't be that mentally inept; after all, she had wrestled control of her financial resources back from her father. And what rich resources they were! Enough to buy Wildwood and set up a nature reserve and still have lots left over. Hopefully, one day her mother would be well enough to leave the house and come to Muskoka to see what her gift had created.

Meanwhile, there was no need to tell anyone who the benefactor was. The intrigue of it could be added to the list of other unsolved mysteries. Like who The Loon was. If it even was one person. For all she knew, Harley might have done the stump, Elfy might have let the mice loose, Joey might have tarred Price's dock. Or a variety of other combinations. But then, maybe it wasn't any of them. As Jessie often said: you could never always sometimes tell.

She glanced down at the black Jaguar again and imagined the woman staring at the bumper of the car in front of her. And here she was, up in the air, free as a bird. If there was one thing she'd learned from flying it was this: perspective changed everything.

• • •

The leaves were shouting with colour when Sushi finally flew in a circle above them, then rose over the trees near Wildwood and headed south down some invisible highway of wind.

"I think that's the last time we'll see him," Harley said.

With a sad smile, Jessie watched until he was out of her range of vision. Would he return in the spring with the other migrating birds? There was no way of knowing. She would miss him, but the thought of him being out in the wild, warmed her.

Ahead of her, Gumption floated on the lake, staring after Sushi.

"Must be frustrating," she said to him. "All those flying lessons and you can't quite make it happen."

Gumption flapped his wings indignantly and prepared to make another attempt.

She could feel the intensity of his effort. This time his exertion was tremendous, and he managed to generate greater speed as he raced across the surface of the water. She winced as he began to wobble, but the sheer force of his determination straightened him out and then, suddenly, up he went, into the sky.

"He made it," Harley said softly. "He's home."

The sound of their cheers flew into the air after him.

Poems cited throughout the book:

Pg. 4
"I thank you God for most this amazing day..." —I Thank You God for Most this Amazing Day by e. e. cummings

Pg. 36
"Meanwhile, the wild geese high in the clear blue air are heading home again. Whoever you are, no matter how lonely, the world offers itself to you, calls to you like the wild geese, harsh and exciting, over and over again, announcing your place..." —Wild Geese by Mary Oliver.

Pg. 46
"And I will arise and go now, and go to Innisfree, and a small cabin build there of clay and wattles made . . ." —The Lake Isle of Innisfree by William Butler Yeats

Pg. 65
"World is suddener than we fancy it, . . . crazier and more of it than we think, incorrigibly plural..." —Snow by Louis MacNeice

Pg. 79
"You only have to let the soft animal of your body love what it loves..." —Wild Geese by Mary Oliver

Pg. 105
"Because I love there is an invisible way across the sky, birds travel that way..."
—Because I Love by Kathleen Raine

Pg.214
"All the sun long, it was running, it was lovely, the hay fields high as the house, the tunes from the chimneys, it was air and playing, lovely and watery..." —Fern Hill by Dylan Thomas